More Like Not Running Away

More Like Not Running Away

a novel

Paul Shepherd

Winner of the 2004
Mary McCarthy Prize in Short Fiction
Selected by Larry Woiwode

Sarabande Books
LOUISVILLE, KENTUCKY

SECOND PRINTING

Managing Editor
Sarabande Books, Inc.
2234 Dundee Road, Suite 200
Louisville, KY 40205

LIBRARY OF CONGRESS CATALOGING-IN-PUBLICATION DATA

Shepherd, Paul, 1960–
        More like not running away : a novel / by Paul Shepherd.— 1st ed.
            p.   cm.
        "Winner of the 2004 Mary McCarthy Prize in Short Fiction."
        ISBN 1-932511-28-8 (pbk. : acid-free paper)
        1. Boys—Fiction. 2. Runaway wives—Fiction. 3. Problem
families—Fiction. 4. Fathers and sons—Fiction. 5. Maternal
deprivation—Fiction. I. Title.
    PS3619.H4573M67 2005
    813'.6—dc22   2005005743

13-digit ISBN: 978-1-932-51128-4

Cover and text design by Charles Casey Martin

Manufactured in the United States of America
This book is printed on acid-free paper.

Sarabande Books is a nonprofit literary organization.

Partial funding has been provided by the Kentucky Arts Council, a
state agency in the Commerce Cabinet, with support from the National
Endowment for the Arts.

This book could only be dedicated to Lois Shepherd.
We've gotten used to each other.

Acknowledgments

Thank you—

To my parents, Joan Hurt and Marion Shepherd, who gave me a love of reading, a love of places, and a love of work. You are not the mother and father of this book, but your lives have inspired me. And to my extended parents Terry Hurt, Martha Shepherd, and Jason and Carolyn Lineberger for years of faithful support.

And to Melanie, Mark, Raney, Jon, David, and Denise. And to all my family, for running with me.

To my teachers and advisors who befriended, especially Miss Ensing and Miss VanderBie, Rebecca Brown, Lee Zacharias, Hunt Hawkins, Van Brock, and Janet Burroway, especially for letting me run away from class; to Dorian Karchmar; to Florida State University for the Kingsbury Fellowship; to Larry Woiwode, a believer; to the Sarabandistas Kristina, Kirby, Sarah, Jeff, Betsey, and Nickole, all for running with this book.

To friends near and far who didn't run, even when I did, who advised and taught: Frank and Kim Garcia, John Masters, Father John Oetgen, Adam Johnson, Beth Watzke, Michael Parker, John Rowell, Thomas Joiner, William McPherson, Tad Hixson, Catherine Reid, Holly Iglesias, Dave Scott, Julianna Baggott, Sheila Curran, Carla Reid and my Black Dog friends, and Geoff Brock; and to the workshop Toni, Mac, John, Andrea, Clark.

To Max Steele and Jane Perrin, who between them saved my life.

To my children, Max, Summer, and Charlie, for how you run to meet me.

And to Lois, who believed when I didn't. You made this right. My best reader, most honest critic, and kindest friend. This has been a marathon you didn't have to run, but you did.

Chapter One published by *Beloit Fiction Journal* in 2002 as "Falling Up"

Chapter Two published by *U.S. Catholic* in 2003 as "People in China"

Chapter Fifteen published by *Crazyhorse* in 2005 as "Always Order What You Want"

Chapter Sixteen published by *Fiction* in 2002 as "More Like Not Running Away"

Introduction

You have in your hands a haunting novel. Levi Revel, the young narrator of *More Like Not Running Away*, hears voices and sounds through walls and floors and electrical sockets and the forces of nature. One voice infuses him with such majesty he preaches from treetops and rooftrees, literally, imagining he's hearing the voice of God. He isn't, of course, and I leave it to you to find whose voice it is in one of the many hair-raising revelations that lie ahead. The story unfolds in the oral, ventriloquial tradition (as in *Huckleberry Finn, The Catcher in the Rye*, and *To Kill a Mockingbird*), a recounting the narrator has rehearsed so many times on his tongue it has the feel of a legend.

The opening scenes of voices streaming through Levi give a sense of how the novel works. Once you feel secure in your perspective on the characters, you're unseated, left as unsettled as the Revel family, the occupants of our attention, when they are uprooted and moved to yet another geophysical location—Florida, Vermont, Arizona, Michigan—by their father, Everest. He is the swaying mast above the well-built craft of this novel.

Although the book's surefooted forward momentum is propelled by its examination of the ways in which borderline families cohere and endure, or do not, in modern America, it hinges on sonship and fatherhood.

Everest Revel is a presence you will not forget, one of the most terrifying fathers I've encountered in recent American writing. Contemporary fictional fathers are often bumbling and ineffective, are worthy only of griping about and consigning to the background, or are merely dismissed. Not so here. The terror Everest inspires is amplified by his wisdom and artful proficiency at dozens of skills, and his dedication to his family. We tremble at their inability to let him go, until we ultimately enter the terrible love of a child for a mother or father, and the nearly messianic obsession a child takes on to care for and to try to correct a wayward parent, up to the turning point when the child becomes a parent to the adult. More pertinent to the story: when a child is willing to risk his life for a parent.

Everest is a bright and resourceful perfectionist, and this is his downfall. He's a carpenter, often the foreman or overseer of a crew, and he hates all shoddy building, can spot the slightest flaw in workmanship, which leads to frustration, at the least; the best carpenter can never attain perfection. At the worst it leads to Everest's decision to build a house of his own, on his own, and the horrendous end to all that.

We come to understand how the schedules and patterns of occupations are the religion of America, in the quest for the American Dream, the ritual of each job's tasks and food and coffee breaks and quitting times as formalized as liturgy. Success is God, material wealth its incarnation, the job The Way or The Path. Intimations of this religion arrive subtly through the book, along with a frontal view of those consigned by society, due to their place of birth or lack of education or lack of success, to the outer circles of the damned.

None of the above suggests the Trans-American feel of the novel, narrated in a purged, cross-continental voice, with the lilt and sonorous inflections of the South in its undertow. Each sentence is so clearly conceived not one misleads or loses the reader; every action runs clear and unblurred to its right conclusion. The book brims with the poetry of the working class, seldom sung lyrics of working men and women whose tasks of constructive creation give them glimpses of a larger order that every pattern they complete echoes, until the exultation of discovery pours into the work as they see in their own minds an even more majestic form.

I remember a story from years ago, narrated by an itinerant laborer, that shifts at its end to a vertiginous essayistic appeal to the reader to set aside prejudice and remain open-minded to people of all kinds, and then noted that a reviewer said it was inconceivable for a common laborer to think in such terms. This is an attitude that needs revision, and *More Like Not Running Away* comes far down the road toward that. The inherent depth in such workmen is observed, without prejudice, in this first novel by Paul Shepherd, which is one of its many glories.

Over and over moments of resolution occur, but no grand, oversimplified, unified solution of uplifting sweetness emerges, no tied-in-a-bow conclusion, no squaring up of the ramshackle structure we sometimes make of our lives, improvising and patching things up as we go—only a sense of how life goes on with bittersweet acceptance, the taste it has always had on Levi's tongue, now with deeper dimensions added. Yet the prose is filled also with celebration, of nature, of the specificity of place in the U.S., of family ties and the will to endure, so that even fear and terror are endured. Or so it is for Levi. As for his father, his mother, his sister Carson, her horse—

For that, turn to the first page of this novel and enter an extraordinary world.

—Larry Woiwode, July 1, 2004

"For a mere moment I have forsaken you,
But with great mercies I will gather you.
With a little wrath I hid my face from you,
for a moment,
But with everlasting kindness I will have mercy on you,"
says the Lord, your Redeemer.

—Isaiah 54: 7–8

part **One**

I have heard things all my life. Whether I want to or not, they come to me, from walls and floors, from places I've been. Growing up, I heard that my dad had done things to be locked away, but for a long time I didn't know what they were.

Even now, when I'm going to say what I found out, the sound of my own blood makes it hard to put the words together.

Falling Up

THE FIRST TIME I HEARD SOMEONE PREACHING, when I was six, the words stuck in me like nails. It was the kind of story my dad would like, how the world would leave a man alone to die, laugh at him, spit on him, call him a liar. But not kill him, not really. And there on the cross the man says *why hast thou forsaken me.* That's when I knew, it was right there in the preacher's red eyes, that I was hearing things for a reason.

"The best part," I told my dad at lunch afterwards, "is how he even tried to help the guys next to him on the cross."

His jaw locked. "I know all about it." His voice came from every corner of the room, but he wasn't yelling. "You want to go there, your mother can take you. I don't like to see a church bus out front of my house," he said. "This isn't a trailer park."

My mom moved her plate to one side and pointed at nothing in particular on the table. "He rode the bus because his friend does. You can't tell the kid not to go to church,

17

More Like Not Running Away

Everest." She was talking to the water in her glass. The part about my friend wasn't exactly true, the kid who invited me wasn't what you'd call a friend, but it didn't matter, not enough to say anything.

"I didn't tell him not to go," my dad said. "I don't keep a Firebird on cinder blocks out in the front yard, and I don't want a mission bus stopping here either. I saw all I wanted of those a long time ago."

I don't think he meant to knock over the glass of water— he was just swinging his hand while he talked—but then before we could even move to stop the water from spreading, he swept everything in front of him to the floor. My mom and my little sister Carson jumped from the noise, but I sat still. I already knew he was going to do it beforehand, and I was listening to how long it took the dishes to break, to how many different ways they broke.

He had gravel in his voice now. "You go wherever you want," he said, not looking at me, "and you get there how-ever you want. All I'm asking is that the bus stay clear of my front door."

I took my napkin from my lap and went outside. We had just moved there, so I hadn't climbed all the trees yet, but I knew which one I was going to. At that time I had never fallen, no matter what I climbed. I'd been to the top of chain-link backstops and swing ropes, and everywhere I went my feet never made a mistake. I went up into a sugar maple that still had a crown of colored leaves. The fear that was quick behind my knees and the cold edges of the air went away when I got to a comfortable place to stand. Our house was far away from anyone else's, and from up there the houses and roads and cars were no more than toys. My dad was right, I could see cars parked in people's front yards. There were other things that were wrong too, like the aluminum siding, the chain-link fences, the crooked mobile homes. If I had wanted, I could have straightened up the yards, squared the roads, lined up the houses, just with my finger.

Instead, I leaned back against the trunk of the tree, raised my arms, and a knot that I didn't know was in me came loose. "It was mean," I said, shaking my words like the preacher had. "It was murder. But he gave his only son!" I knew every word, when to pause, even how to lower my eyes. When I got to the part about him hanging on the cross, I showed my palms. It was my voice, but I didn't have to think of the words, not even to try to remember them: the whole sermon came through me like I was a radio.

When my mom came out, her hands were red from the dishwater. I wanted to say the part about the nails again, but she started talking first. "Levi, you're going to fall out of that tree if you don't hold on." She didn't really mean it, she knew better. "What are you talking about anyway? Who are you talking to?"

I didn't even look down. "It was like splinters, only worse," I said. "They were nails. And they went all the way through." Through, through, through, I could hear the words landing inside her.

"Listen," she said, "what happened in the house, you know, he would never do anything to hurt you. He's never laid a hand on any of us."

"I'm going to build a church here. On this branch. Can you buy some boards?"

But she wasn't listening. She shook her head. "Do you hear what I'm saying, Levi? When you run out of the house like that, it just makes things worse."

I let my arms down. "He makes things worse," I said.

More Like Not Running Away

"Well," she said, "he's a good man, he loves you." She took her hair from her eyes. "You're what keeps him together. He can't stand to think that you'd go through any of the things he went through, that's all."

He was so poor when he was growing up that for a few years, they all lived on the back porch of a mill house. That's what she meant. My mom left then. She was as beautiful as a person could be, and she could make people laugh even when they didn't want to. I preached some more after she left. I stayed up in the tree so long that when I let my foot down, my leg felt dead. My arms, too, were empty of strength from preaching with them. I wondered, just for a moment, if I was stuck in the tree, but it was only a moment, then I was inching my way down, making every move just perfectly, like I was being held by invisible hands.

He came by my room later in the afternoon. I'd been building with blocks or something, mainly just listening over and over to the choir from that morning, to how their voices had gone in so many directions at once, but had not come apart.

"Listen," he said, "come on outside with me." The way he said it so perfectly, like I was the only person in the world, I would have walked with him into a furnace. He didn't say anything more until we were in the gravel driveway near his truck. He motioned me in. It was an old truck, a Chevy Cheyenne with a bench seat I could lie down on. On Saturday afternoons when he took me to the jobsites, I'd take naps there, going to sleep to the steady drone of a backhoe or the slow sound of his pencil drawing out something on the hood of the truck.

"Let's go," he said.

"Where to?"

"Nowhere. Just nowhere." He didn't head up the road, though, he went farther down the driveway to the edge of the field where I'd been in the tree. He stopped.

"You drive." He waved me to him. He lifted me into his lap and put my hands to the steering wheel. I thought we were going to just pretend, like I did sometimes, but then he let the truck start moving. I didn't want to say anything because I was afraid he'd move me off, that he wasn't really going to let me steer. But he did. Even though there wasn't a path to drive on, he headed the truck into the field. The thrill of it, of actually steering the truck myself, opened in me all at once, like a bird had beat its wings in my chest. I still didn't dare speak, so I tried to figure if there was anywhere I was supposed to drive, but still there wasn't a road so I guessed I just had to stay away from the fences and trees. He touched the gas a bit. I turned one way, then another, just amazed that I could move something so enormous with nothing but my hands.

I remember that he lit a cigarette while we were doing this, and that's when I knew that it was all going to be okay. He'd lay a hand on the wheel now and then, but he never jerked it away, he'd just guide me around a hole or rock I hadn't seen. He probably said something to me—something about how I was going to do a great thing, or how the world could be hard for a kid like me, he said things like that, he knew things about me that I didn't even know—but maybe not, maybe we just went around the field that day, again and again, and we were just quiet.

I loved these things about that time: his legs moving under me to push the pedals like I was riding a horse; the grownup smell of that cigarette, almost like I was having a little of it too; and of course having the wheel in my hands.

———

More Like Not Running Away

Later that night they were talking through my bedroom wall. "He needs to get to know somebody," my mom said. "We've dragged him from one end of the country to another." Her words came through the wires, out of the plugs.

My dad had slow words. "This family's never had to do without. We'll have the money to set up in a real house before long. Somewhere where we're not surrounded by a bunch of goddamn factory stiffs."

"It's not just the moving."

My dad knew, though. "He might as well learn now as later, if people want to keep a distance, let them," he said. "I provide a decent home." His voice went lower now, till I could only make out a few of the words, but I knew exactly what he was saying. The next place we moved to, we'd stay longer, through the whole school year. He'd find us land, and start building a house, the way a house should be built. We just needed to be where people left him alone.

For a while it was quiet downstairs. They laughed, but not out loud. "I'll take him to church from now on," my mom said. "At least there he'll have a place, someplace he can relate to. I guess."

We moved and moved again, and moved again. I kept going to churches, wherever we lived, and in all of them God talked to me from the rafters, through the floors, in words that never quite became words, saying all the things I would do. I heard my mom and dad talking, fighting, getting ready for our next sudden move. The closeness of their voices made the nights familiar. Every place we went, I kept climbing, and preaching, waiting to hear a secret, a secret that I knew they were trying to bury.

———

When I was twelve we moved to Holland, Michigan. My mom said she loved the flatness of the land there, the small, proud houses with their just-right gardens. "I could live here," she said, "even in one of those Dutch neighborhoods." But every time we moved, we went further away from other people, and this time we rented an old farmhouse at the end of a dirt road.

More than anywhere else we'd lived, this house itself seemed to be constantly moving. Every door scraped when it shut, the pipes groaned all night, and even when we were asleep, something would hiss or knock like it was lost, trying to find its way out. As the winter came on, the cold bones of the house began creaking, the wood pulling from its nails. There were times at night when the wind rattled through my bedroom windowpanes, steady and deliberate. I folded corners of notebook paper to wedge in between the glass and wood, but they worked loose.

One Sunday morning in January I pried the window open and stepped out on to the roof. White flakes of paint fell from the outside ledge to the black shingles. "This is my father's world," I sang out. "He moves in all that's fair; in the rustling grass I hear him pass; he's with me everywhere." This was a very steep roof—I think an 8/12 pitch—and I was barefoot. The shingles were hard from the cold, so the grit kept slipping. It didn't matter because I still had never fallen. By now I'd sneaked up to the top of a small radio tower, and on to the roofs of schools, and walked floor joists and perimeter walls on my dad's jobsites. There were gray birds below me in a dead tree. I held my finger out to the back yard, closed one eye, and sighted the black tree, my dad's pickup, the pasture fence. Over the ridge of the roof, I traced the elevations of the few houses I could see, our neighbors, people we didn't know.

————

More Like Not Running Away

They lived in newer houses with simple gable roofs, with tiny trees in huge front yards. My dad said their houses were put together like *Popular Mechanix* picnic tables. There wasn't any snow right then, and some cornstalks that had not been plowed under glinted in the sun. I had walked everywhere that I could see, even on the other people's property.

"I rest me in the thought," I sang again, "of rocks and trees, of skies and seas, his hand the wonders wrought." I raised my arms. I would speak now, and everything beneath me waited. Downstairs, my dad would be sleeping with his face to the wall, empty after six days of walking walls, pounding nails, and listening to the screech of Skilsaws as he trudged through rivers of muck.

It should have been perfect up there. But the house below me moved, maybe it was just my dad getting up, opening a cabinet door, but my balance was off. No, I knew what it was: Edgar Surface. Whenever someone at a new school picked on me, I could just look at them and they'd back off. My sister Carson said there was something hard in my eyes, like broken glass, that made people stop talking to me. I couldn't help it. But it was different with Edgar. Something in his flat hair and pointed face made me avoid his eyes, so he was constantly taking my hat or wadding up my homework. And flicking me. I ignored him. I said quit. Still he pestered, and now, on the roof, I knew that unless we moved again right away, I'd have to hit him to make him stop.

I fixed my eyes on a distant house to catch my balance. But the door to it opened, and an old man in white pajamas came out muttering, putting down each foot like it hurt. His loneliness against all the flat land and the cold sky and his cemetery walk made me feel sorry for him. I put up my hand. *May the Lord make his face to shine on you,* I said.

The man started talking. At first, his words just vanished, but then they got louder, jamming together, coming not just from him but everywhere all at once. Thousands of leaves joined in, tree branches thudded against each other, and the wind screamed into my ears. Other voices piled in, voices I knew and voices I'd never imagined, all choking me. I tried to say something, but my own voice went back down my throat. I didn't even know if I was still standing up, or if I was falling.

Then my foot did slip. I almost went over backwards, but I caught myself. I tried to cover my ears, but that made my balance even worse.

Finally I shook my head side to side. The noises softened, until they were no more than muffled notes from a song, a bird brushing the air. It worked, I kept nodding. I went to the peak and sat, straddling it. I wouldn't have been surprised if the trees below me were uprooted or buildings blown down, but no, the brown grass was still empty, waiting for snow. Carson mumbled in her sleep, my mom set a pot of coffee on the stove. The old man's words sorted out; he said I was going to fall. I know that now, it was the only thing he could have said.

The sun had warmed the roof by the time I heard the gravel scratching in the driveway. I caught just the tail section of my Aunt Frankie's red and white Dodge Charger as it pulled into the driveway, its glasspack muffler beating the air. I hadn't seen her in over a year, when she'd surprised me for my eleventh birthday, but I remembered her exact shade of lipstick, the white leather car seats, and the drug store perfume she kept in the glove box. My mom always said that Frankie was hot enough to burn herself to death, if she ever lost her cool. She'd run away from home and been married twice, but didn't have any kids. She and my mom would laugh and whisper at the kitchen table, past midnight, telling stories and crying and arguing. Now Frankie was right below me, at the front door. She always said that back doors were for dogs and naughty children. She was wrapped up in a black and gold striped outfit.

"You look like a tiger, Frankie." I stood over the front stoop.

She gasped. "Oh Levi, it's you," she said. She held one hand over her eyes. "And you look like a steeple. So where's all the people?" She winked.

"Inside."

"What are you doing up there? What if you fall?"

"You fall up."

She cocked her head. "Well, I may not be as smart as your mom, but I know that you fall down, not up." She always said she was the only one who knew how smart my mom was.

"But you fall up a roof. You have to think about what could go wrong, and know which way to fall."

"Sounds a lot like it is down here. When did you get a horse?" She pointed behind the house.

"This summer. Her name's Delilah. She bites."

"Ooh. Great name for a horse. Especially one who bites." Suddenly she didn't look like a tiger anymore, she just gave a little cough and went in the house.

Inside they started talking, their voices sawing. Frankie talked so faintly I could barely make out the words through the shingles. The wind stirred a few branches, but it didn't bother me. Times like that, when the morning was right, with a good sun, usually filled me with so many words, with the poems my dad taught me, with songs, but not today. I let my head roll back and forth again, like I had a little while ago, when the wind was screaming at me, and something in the sideways rocking, in the sliding of my eyes, in the cotton of my skull, something in that motion of my head was just me, musical and quiet at the same time, a little sad, but mainly calm. It took all the sounds outside of me away, but it wasn't lonely. In fact, it was the least lonely thing I'd ever done. A warmness, like the warmness of another person, radiated down my spine, and spread through my abdomen.

The back door of the house slammed. The heavy shape of my dad moved, from the house to his pickup, his shoulders held back hard. His face was sunsoaked even in the winter. I could smell his Pall Mall. He had a thick crop of black hair that curled in the back and did not move in the breeze. He lifted his beaten toolbags from the front seat. His hammer, with the handle as long as my thigh, swung through the open window and the nails clinked. He cinched the belt around his waist, and turned his face to the sun for a breath.

"Don't you fall." The bark of his voice took me by surprise, and I shifted my weight up the roof, almost throwing myself backwards. I was too near the edge—I knew it in my knees.

"I won't. Are you going to work on the stable?" I asked.

He nodded. He started pulling out timbers from the back of his truck, a kind of wood I'd never seen before, with huge sworls and charred streaks from end to end. Everywhere we lived, he built miraculous things, a redwood swingset that spanned a creek, a sleeping loft that could be cranked up and down, suspended from the ceiling by chains, and stair pickets of maple branches hand-mortised into the railings. Things we left behind, things he said he built because no one needed them, because, he said, he could build them without having to talk to jackleg superintendents, architects, or homeowners. Things my mom said we wasted. *All this work,* she'd say, *for*

*who? Who are we leaving these monuments for, the landlords? You
think they're going to want them?*

"You want some help?" I asked.

"In a little while. You can pull the nails out."

"Where's Aunt Frankie? She looked like a tiger."

He let a beam hit the ground. "Yeah, I guess so. Just what
we need." He started bending some of the nails back.

I picked at a loose shingle. "How much would it cost to
buy this house?"

"This?" He yanked out a nail, the board groaning. "This
place needs too much. You'd spend as much fixing it as you
would buying it."

"Even if we did it ourselves?"

He laid his hammer down. "Well, let me tell you. It's what
you don't see that would rob you blind." He jabbed a finger to
the house. "Built by Sears lumber salesmen. The foundation's
settling. The whole place is sinking, an inch at a time. You'd
have to jack it up, repour the footings. By then you've busted
the plaster, messed up the doorjambs, the windows, and
that's before you get to the plumbing, the wiring, shit." He
stubbed out his cigarette.

It was my mom's idea. The night before she'd shown me
the creased, narrow slips of paper striped with colors,
Heather Rose, Early Dawn, Santa Fe Clay. She talked about
the living room walls, even the front door. She pointed to a
picture of curtains in a magazine—wouldn't these dress it up,
she said. Don't laugh, just tell me if it's too, you know,
country. She could do so much of it herself, she was sure, even
getting the mortgage. But one thing, if I would just talk to my
dad about it, he'd listen to me. Maybe I could get him to think
about finally settling down. You've got a way with him, she
said, you know the right words.

Now my dad was turned away, spitting his words, like the whole house was about to fall on him. I knew he was right, at least about the house. I knew what he was saying under his breath, *There are some things you kids, your mother can't understand—the time will come when you all see why I can't just run out and do what you all want me to do. There are things you can't ever understand. I come from . . .* When he lived with his mom and sister on that back porch, they were afraid to open the kitchen door for a drink of water. When he ran away and joined the Army, he still couldn't read. They thought at first he was retarded, till they found out he couldn't read, that he just needed someone to teach him something. When he talked about the Army, he said things happened that made him feel like an animal was crawling in his ear. There were things I didn't know about him, but I knew that when he'd gun his truck down the driveway or tip over the table, what looked out through his eyes was never wild or mad, but still, like he was holding a bullet in his teeth.

"Your mom says some kid's picking on you."

"Not really," I said.

"Well, don't let nobody screw with you. You've got to stop things before they get started." He threw a board to the ground. "How we ended up in this Godforsaken state in the first place."

Actually, this time I knew why we'd moved—I'd seen it. I was in the truck with him, just before he said we were packing up again, when a guy cut him off. We drove after him, so fast I worried that our engine would explode. Eventually the man pulled over and opened his door to get out. My dad drove right alongside him, swiping the door with my side of the truck, jacking the other car's door backwards. The guy jumped just out of the way, but still I wasn't sure if we'd missed him. I tried looking back, but that's when I saw that my window was broken. The next day, my dad said we were going to Michigan.

Around me, brown fields spread apart. The roads, the towns, even the houses around here had acres between them. When the snow came, things were even farther apart, even the empty spaces filled up. The straightness of the roads and the perfect rectangles of the brick ranches on all that flat, square land was not beautiful. But it was not Godforsaken.

"I'll show your mother this afternoon. They're in the truck." His voice was suddenly softer. I realized with a start that I'd been nodding my head, and I didn't know how long he'd been talking. I lost my balance again; my left foot actually slipped out from under me and I gasped, then I fell up, grabbing the ridge.

"What in the hell are you doing?" He shook his head a little.

I stood up quickly. "I slipped. Just a little."

"Well just get down from there. I don't know what in the hell you're doing up there in the first place. You haven't heard a goddamn word I've said to you."

I didn't answer. I didn't move.

He waited, then lit a cigarette. "I said, I sketched a plan out. For your mother. For you and Carson. A house."

"A house? For us?"

"Yes," he yanked a nail. "Yes, I just said that. What are you listening to? The goddamn birds? You damn near busted your ass just now. You don't get up on a roof and draw blanks. Think. Think about where you're at. I'm telling you, we're building a house. I'm building a house. I'll take you all out to see the land I've got in mind this afternoon. You can look at the plans. But I'm telling you, I'm going to need your help. You're old enough now to make a difference. But by God, you're going to have to learn how to listen."

From the ground, he talked of the cathedral ceilings, the tile in the kitchen, the dishwasher, the solid six-panel doors, all trimmed in hardwood, held up with mahogany beams, paneled in walnut (always walnut) and cypress, handmade brick, Andersen windows. He knew the secrets of his trade, how to pick the materials, how to make it all happen: a house cantilevered on every side, a building bigger than its foundation. Even after he left, I said his words over and over in my mouth, the hardwoods and stones, the ivy, the land itself.

I had climbed on the roof to preach a sermon to the trees and grass that someone else owned, to leave for whoever lived there after us. To pretend. And always before when my dad talked about building for us, I somehow knew it would be somewhere else, some other time. But the land he promised to show me now was real, the house he would build now was a real thing, and he would really need my help.

Hungry Everywhere

THAT NIGHT, MY MOM AND FRANKIE talked late in the kitchen. I finally got out of bed, and came downstairs. They held their coffee cups the same way, tightly, close to their faces. They had spread my dad's drawings of the new house out on the table between them. The wind slipping through the windows and under the kitchen door wasn't cold, but I poured myself a cup of coffee anyway.

"It's past midnight," my mom said, pulling out a chair for me. "I guess you heard us."

"Mom didn't tell us you'd be coming," I said to Frankie.

"Well," Frankie said, "I had some business in Muskegon." Her business always changed, but always brought her a town away from where we were living.

She reached over and tapped my ribs. "He's your ace in the hole. I can tell. I've known a few guys like this one in my day," she said. She left her finger barely touching me. "But they usually carry a little more weight around the middle by the time I come across them."

The way she touched me lingered, faint and electric under my skin, for a long time after she quit. "I always said, this boy's built like a baseball player. So," she said to me, "tell me. When do I get to see you play, then?"

"I can't ever hit the ball," I said. People were always trying to get me to play baseball. I did it a few times, mainly in P.E., but it was always the same. I could feel the throwing and catching and hitting in my bones, so easy, like the game was a machine that I fit into. But then the talk started; kids picking, or joking, or just talking the way they do, that constant, needling flybuzz. Their voices linked up in a wall that I couldn't see through. When that happened, and it always happened, no matter how I moved it was like swimming through sand.

Frankie stood up and stretched out her arm. Her red nails waved me closer. "Let me show you," she said. "I've seen enough to know something, anyway." She bent her knees, held up her elbows, and leaned into a stance. The tiger dress and her tangerine shoes made her look ready to jump out the door. "Stand just so," she said, then she drew a line in the air from her eyes. "And watch the ball. That's where all the problems start. You think you watched it. But you didn't. Watch it all the way, till your bat comes out and gets it." She slid back into her seat, nodding. "Do that," she tapped my knee, "and the girls, well, they'll never know what hit them."

One thing about Frankie, she always made it seem like talking to other kids would be so easy. In some ways, she seemed to know me better than anyone else—like now, talking about baseball, right when we'd just played it in P.E., and right when it seemed like all the other kids knew something about it that I didn't. And I'd struck out, in front of Edgar, and he'd sneered about it all day.

"Oh Frankie," my mom said, "don't embarrass him." She shook a finger at Frankie and turned to me. "She did that all the time when we were growing up. She'd say things, right in front of my friends—in front of boys, even! She just wants to see you squirm." She turned to Frankie. "He plays his cards pretty close to the chest," she said. "But then, he's got a pretty good hand. He knows how to keep everyone guessing, that's for sure."

"Well," Frankie said, "here's what I'm guessing. He knows more about this new house than he's letting on, don't you, Sport? And all these details! This ship's window in the attic, can you imagine? The whole thing, it's fun, and it's still beautiful at the same time." She took out a long cigarette and squeezed her eyes shut. Her eyelashes were thick and shiny. "I can see you there, hon," she said. "I just hope, just that," she poured herself more coffee, even though her cup was almost full. "I don't really know anything about construction. It just seems like there's so many things that get mixed up, you know?"

My mom lit a Pall Mall and nodded to me. "So what do you have to say? Is this all your idea?"

"Did you see this part?" I asked, pointing to the drawings. "Do you know what this is?"

They looked at each other, then shook their heads. "We were just wondering that before you came in," my mom said.

"It's a courtyard," I said. "You knew that, right? And some planters, you know, for plants, that's what these lines are for. But right here, in this corner, that's his favorite part of the whole thing. He says it's a water garden, with a real fountain coming over some rocks, built right into the patio. That's what those things are, rocks. That's how you draw them on a plan. And see this dotted line? That's a gas line, you know, like for a stove. And it goes right under one of these flat rocks, you can't really see it exactly the way it is here, but he explained it to me. I said he should think about having it branch off, right here, and have a little gas flame that's always burning, right in the fountain. That was my idea. He said he'd think about it, too."

"Well," said Frankie, "I'll just be. Would that cost a lot?"

"You know," my mom said, "they used to say Everest was retarded when he was a kid. Now you look at this and tell me, if that doesn't just go to show you how wrong people are about him. Even I was wrong," she said. "I'd just about given up on him. I thought we were going to spend the rest of our lives trucking around the country from job to job, moving in and out of other people's houses." She lit another cigarette and pointed to her temple. "But he's got a way of knowing, a way of seeing. And I'll tell you something," she said, "when he gets this place built, all someone's going to have to do is come and see it, and they'll know, he's the one they want building their houses.

"Slapping up those tract houses and apartment complexes year after year for those developers, it drives him crazy. I don't think he even realizes how much running from place to place is just running away from having to spend day after day doing other people's lousy work."

She bubbled up like that whenever Frankie visited. She stayed up late, raised her arms, talked fast, and tapped the table with her finger. As long as I could remember, whenever I woke up in the middle of the night she would be there, at the kitchen table, with a pot of coffee, ready to talk for an hour, no matter if it was bedtime or not. If it was raining or snowing it was perfect. There was something about the wide darkness all around us, the quiet. Sometimes she cried about things. She wondered if we'd ever stay somewhere long enough to get to know people. But she laughed a lot too. She told me stories about tricks she used to play on my dad when they first got married and lived in a shoebox apartment, when I was born.

It was quiet now for a while, then Frankie said "Men can be restless." She seemed to be thinking a long way away.

"I was restless myself for the best part of my life," my mom answered. "Everything was so plain when we were growing up. I know I keep talking about it like it was something bad, but you know, I got to where I didn't think I could breathe another breath of that same old air."

"Well," Frankie laughed, "you sure found someone who won't let the air get stale." She turned to me. "The day your mom brought him home—she didn't tell us she'd been married. The first time he opened his mouth my heart stopped. We never had those Southern manners around, the 'sir' and 'ma'am' in the sugary voice. He'd been in some kind of trouble, of course, you could tell in his eyes. Restless. Men are that way."

"We've even had good fights," my mom said. "Fights that were fun to make up from. He thought I was dead once. I really thought I had him. I thought, if that SOB is going to storm out of here like that, I'll teach him a lesson. I'd seen the catsup trick in some movie, I think. So when he pulled up in the driveway, I was laughing so hard I almost forgot how mad I was. It wasn't funny, really," she said, nodding to me like it was my fault. "I drizzled the catsup down my neck, right down the front of a brand-new blouse. Ruined it. And there I am, dead as a doornail at the bottom of the stairs and a butcher knife with catsup all over it in my hand, and what does he do? He walks in with a handful of flowers he'd pulled in the park. I just knew I had him. He acts tough, but I knew if he thought I'd killed myself it would have scared the daylights out of him."

She dragged her thumb across her lip. She moved the cigarette like an evil movie star walking out on a guy. "He didn't so much as give me a second look. He sets the flowers on the table like he walks over dead bodies every day. So I let out a little gurgling noise, you know, like there's blood in my throat or something. Nothing, not a word. 'You know,' he says finally when he steps over me on his way up the stairs, 'next time you try this you should hide the catsup bottle. Then you won't look like a damned leftover French fry.'"

She smiled. The smoke from her cigarette curled against the coffee cup. "Taught me," she said. "What to look for when you find a body, anyway." They started laughing, but my mom caught herself, she even put her hand up to her mouth like she wanted to take back something she'd said, but then she laughed again.

"He'll build you the best house in the world," Frankie said. "You'll help him too, won't you?" She put her hand on mine. "It took me two marriages to figure out how hard it is to get a man to settle down. But some men, they just can't help running, running after something, away from something. Just running, I guess."

Later that night I still did not sleep. I lay in the stillness of my room, hearing only my own short, uneven breaths. Soft pictures of the house we'd build faded in and out, and I could actually hear the perfect silence of it—our own quiet place. I thought I heard my dad saying something and I couldn't sort out whether he was really talking to me there in the bedroom or if I was dreaming it. He was saying something he'd said before, that he hoped someday God would talk to him, too, because as far as he knew, God couldn't hear a damn thing. The place where Frankie had touched me now ached, but not like anything had ever ached on me before; this was a hunger just of my skin that tingled from my throat to my groin. If I stopped thinking about it, it quieted, but then it would come back again. I imagined the nakedness of myself, and of other people, under their clothes, and mixed these with other pictures—of the rivers of kids from the schools I'd been to, nameless and faceless and murmuring, of Jesus weeping, of myself preaching. When I put my hand to the place Frankie had touched, my own skin felt strange, then it became electric again, weakening me, the way laughing would, when it was mixed with fear. Finally I rocked my head back and forth, back and forth, into the deepest silence I could find.

"I don't get it." My sister Carson ran her hand along Delilah's mane. It made Delilah shiver and it made me shiver. Carson was ten then, with chopped up hair she cut herself and muscles like a boy. She was a kid like other kids I knew, except I'd known her longer than a year. "How can you move a whole stable? Why doesn't he just build the stable there, at the new house?"

She didn't actually believe we'd get the house built. I drew an outline of the stable framework in the dirt with a stick. "This is all it is," I said. "It just rests right on the ground, on these things like runners. It doesn't even need a floor. They can lift it right up with a forklift. Then they stick it in the back of a truck and take it to the new house." I waited for her to nod. She held her face to Delilah's, then wiped out the drawing with her toe. "Anyway," I said, "he can't start building anything on the new land until we get a loan approved. It's a lot of stuff you wouldn't understand. So this is something he can start building now. He's building it mainly for you, you know. Nobody else in this family could care less if we had a horse."

She narrowed her eyes. "I don't care what kind of house you all build," she snapped, "that's all anybody cares about around here. This kind of wood and that kind of wood, and how big it is. It's stupid." Her hair would have looked bad on almost any girl but her. She had that smile—you could see her teeth, kind of crooked, but people loved it. "Other families aren't like this one," she rasped. "They talk about normal things."

She didn't understand. That was always the problem with Carson. Whenever we started at a new school the other kids acted like they already knew her. She'd start talking about all the places we lived and made it sound like we were some kind of world travelers. Even animals liked her, even birds. She carried a bag of sunflower seeds in her backpack and she'd go on the playground and throw them out and then birds would come up, then kids would come up. She could ride Delilah so easy, too, always moving her legs just right, barely tugging the reins. It was like a string ran through her and other kids and animals. And she didn't ever care if the rest of the family had a hold of the string or not.

"It's not just a house," I said. "It's not just wood. You should hear Mom—"

"Mom's had a suitcase, packed up, in the closet ever since we moved here. She doesn't want what you want, what you and dad want. She just wants to live somewhere long enough to get to know somebody. That's what you don't get. It's like you don't even hear her. She's losing it, and you don't even know it. You watch. If Dad screws this house up, if he starts lying and talking big all the time, she's leaving him. She said it. You go look in the closet." Carson shrugged. "Not like it matters to me anyway."

She made it sound so right, but I knew a hundred ways she was wrong. She would never listen, she'd never understand. She didn't really believe in the house, she didn't believe in God, she didn't believe in anything except the stupid girls she sat with on the bus. I thought of the girls on the bus, of the place we lived in Colorado where the red sand had turned to stone, and of all the places we'd lived. I knew my mom was tired of moving, but she'd never leave my dad.

"Delilah needs water. From the spring," Carson said. "The water from the hose is too hard."

"You know," I followed her away from the house, toward the trail in the woods, "you act like you know all about people, but you don't. There's things you don't know about, like Dad, and maybe if you'd just listen sometimes to what he says."

She cut her eyes at me. "You're the one who everyone thinks is so weird," she said. "Preaching up in trees and hanging around churches all the time. You make people think you're losing it. Like when you talk about being some kind of missionary in Pakistan or whatever. Like you think that's going to make people like you or something."

The mosquitoes were at me, at the back of my knees. It had been a long time, at least a year, since I'd said anything about the missionary idea, but she just wouldn't leave it alone. She never listened to me, unless I said something like that, and then it was like she knew just how to spit the words back at me. When I first told her about being a missionary, I'd seen the hungry eyes and faces on TV one day, and I thought, I could see myself right there, telling them the truth, saving them. I had read once about people in China, hundreds of thousands of them, who still lived in caves. When I went to sleep, I could hear the way they talked, their strange language like a song, and I understood every word. Later that night a voice from the walls said Go, and my heart beat at the closeness of it. The next night at dinner I told my dad about it and he said he always knew it, that I was being led to do great things in the world. "But," he said, "people everywhere are just like that, hungry just like that. Being poor and hungry doesn't make it any easier to like them. If it did, everyone would be rushing over trying to feed them. Instead, everyone's rushing to get the hell away from them."

Now Carson let the water pail bang against the trees. I stopped to slap at the mosquitoes, leaving traces of blood. I liked Carson. We almost never fought each other, I just couldn't understand why she acted like me and Mom and Dad were so bad. Even now, she didn't wait for me, she just kept walking.

I caught up with her. "You know," I said, "there really are kids like that, who don't have any food. If you saw the pictures like I did—"

She held her eyebrows close together, mocking me. "Oh I know," she said, "they got flies in their eyes. And you're going to build some huge church there, like Jesus is going to keep the flies off. Right."

I didn't answer. If I did, she would know just what to say back, that's how she was, like the other kids.

The spring at the bottom of the hill was almost too perfect. I wished for a minute we could drag sticks in the water, or drop leaf boats down the stream, but she turned to leave.

"You know," I said, "I didn't say anything about building a church."

Then, instead of leaving, she stopped and sat down next to me. "You didn't have to," she said. She made a leaf boat, and dropped it in the water. After a while, she said, "You know, you need some friends. You should invite somebody over sometime. How come you never do that? Everyone else does, you know. It's weird not to."

When she looked at me, I knew, she was sorry. "I mean, if we're actually going to stay here—I mean *if*—and we have this new house and all, you should start hanging out with somebody. Somebody—" she looked into the trees, "cute. Like Jacob VanderBier. I mean, if we stay here long enough, you're going to have to make some kind of friend."

Then a wonderful thing happened. Even though the water pails were full and even though I had to keep slapping mosquitoes away, Carson and I played. Maybe it was only for an hour, but I think it was longer, maybe for the rest of the afternoon. We loaded a dozen leaf boats with sand, all they could carry, and they never sank. I even took off my shoes and splashed my feet in the icy water. I didn't hear anything special, I didn't think about anything, it was just like that day when I was steering the truck, I was just there, just right. I remember Carson spent a long time digging out a little pool for some little fish she'd found, and I built an island out of some rocks, big enough for me to actually sit on.

"What's with that kid on the bus who flicks you," she said.

"Nothing."

"I'll make him quit," she said.

"Just leave it," I said. "I can handle it."

When we were walking back up the hill, she told me about a time I'd forgotten, when she was in kindergarten, when a boy was picking on her at the playground and I'd come up and poked my finger right in his chest.

"You said if he didn't leave me alone you were going to be all over him like white on rice. You said that, white on rice. I think you'd heard Dad say it." She reached over and poked

More Like Not Running Away

me in the side, playing, and I put my hand on her shoulder. For a while after that I'd say the words to myself, white on rice, trying to remember how I would have actually said them, and how I might have pulled my shoulders back, but I couldn't. It didn't matter, though. I believed her.

A Wall

MY DAD KNEW ALL ABOUT PLACES. He'd found places for us to rent that always had something different, like the house on stilts over a river, or the octagon, or the log house in Maine that didn't even have electricity. The land he picked for our new house was set back from the road with so many trees you couldn't see in. A streambed ran right along where he wanted to build. He'd changed the plans so the house would cantilever over the water.

The first day I worked there with him, we cut brush for the drive. He swung the machete and I carried away what he cut down, neither of us talking for a time. I imagined the lumber trucks grinding down the road, the piles of lumber around the site, the muscles I would have from carrying boards. My dad and I would cut beams from single trees, so heavy that it would take all our strength to heave them into place, but they would still fit perfect. People would be amazed at the

45

construction, wondering how we ever picked up the beams, saying that the house would last forever, that we'd all die before it fell down. I would walk the tops of the joists, my feet moving like my dad's, never missing a step. I would sweat like him, and our sweat would drip into the wood of the walls and floors, and even when I was an old man I would come back to the house and know that, where no one could see, we had left our marks.

"Later," he said at last, "I need you to go to the bank with me. We got to actually close the loan today. Believe it or not, we're still on somebody else's land here."

"What if they don't sign it or something? Then what would we do?"

He drove his machete into a limb. "They'll sign," he said. "You don't need to worry about that. It's just a lot of goddamn paperwork." He waved his hand across the land. "That's what banks do. They don't give a shit if you're building something that's going to fall down in ten years or not. Just so you sign all their papers.

"Your mother, I don't know if she understands that. She thinks I'm designing some kind of monument, some kind of dream."

I could see it, and I know that's why he wanted me, not her, to go to the bank with him. He walked to the truck, kicking up little clouds of dust from his boots, pulled out a set of blueprints, and spread them out on the hood. "You could do this on a napkin at a Howard Johnson's," he said, "but a blueprint is a napkin with an education. They like blueprints at the bank. Makes them think they're not just dealing with some cracker from North Carolina."

I stood on the front bumper. I knew which lines were the walls, where the windows were, the door arcs. But some lines turned, ending and beginning, crossing one another, in dots and dashes, with circles, and squares, and symbols with numbers in them. "What are these?" I pointed to one of the symbols.

"Hm?" He traced a line, a wall, then shook his head.

"These things, shaped like this. What are they for?"

"Well, those lines are walls." He wasn't looking where my hand was.

"I know that. And I know the doors and windows and all. But what about this?"

"That? That's for the electrician. So he knows where to put the wires, what gauge to use, where the outlets are, what kind of outlets."

"Don't you get confused sometimes?"

He stared hard at the blueprint. "Right now," he said, "I can't figure out why he didn't put this door where I told him to. It's too close to the wall. It won't open all the way. That's the kind of thing you want to figure out now, before you've framed it. Then you're tearing shit out. These guys," he said, "these architects screw up all the time. Too much time in school. They need to get out on jobsites, see how things are really built. A hundred years ago, that's what an architect was—a master builder, someone who'd done time on the job, who knew it inside and out. You can't understand a beam span until you've had your hand on the wood, till you've picked it up and dropped it, and listened to it."

In school I would draw imaginary houses, detailed floor plans and front and side elevations. I drew houses three stories tall with chimneys rising up through the roof, circle top windows, and wild combinations of herringbone and soldier courses of brick. Once I drew a house with a round room—even the ceiling and floors were curved—for listening to music. It would be like sitting in an egg. I found ideas in books and magazines, from things my dad showed me, and I always added something impossible. Some had parapets, secret rooms, chases for dumbwaiters, skywindows, libraries with sixteen foot tall bookshelves and rolling ladders, atriums with real trees growing through holes in the floor, courtyards, and always, those cantilevers. My dad loved cantilevers, and wherever we went he pointed them out to me—remarkable balconies, cornices, bridges, and concrete beams. He said a cantilever was the most graceful thing a building could have because it defied everything that pulled a building down. The best ones made you think something was about to collapse.

He always knew, though, what I'd missed—closet space, ventilation patterns, spans, the bearing walls in the wrong place. He pointed now to the blueprint. "A house stands up," he said, locking his fingers, "because of all the things pushing and pulling against each other. The way the walls meet in the corners keeps them from falling. It's the same with the roof. Everything underneath it holds it up, but the weight of the roof keeps everything underneath it from coming loose and sliding apart." He pulled his hands apart. "The same things that make it fall down are the things that keep it standing up."

The way he stood there right then, on land he was about to go put into his name, knowing so much about so many things, I figured that whatever had happened a long time ago was really behind him now. If he really had been running away from something, or if there was still something wrong that I didn't know about, he'd be able to make it right.

He rolled up the blueprints and threw them behind the seat. "Let's go to the goddamn bank," he said.

We spun down the dirt tracks where the driveway would be. Sunlight flashed in my window and I rolled it down. His cigarette smoke came across the cab, clear and gray. The men he worked with always smelled brown and sour from their cigarettes. They crammed them in their mouths, or let them hang from their lips. They hacked, too. But my dad did it right; he held his cigarettes lightly, and raised them to his lips like he cared about them. When he breathed in the smoke, his chest rose easily and he never coughed.

"You worked hard this morning," he said. "Nothing wrong with work. Everyone should have to make a living with his hands sometime. You appreciate what it means to have to fight for a paycheck." He glanced my way. "How old are you now, anyway?"

"Twelve." My hands and arms had started stinging from where the branches scraped them. It felt good. "How old were you when you started working?"

He leaned back in the seat, a hard grin set on his face. "That was different. I'm not talking about you cutting out of school when you're seven years old because your old man's gone too much of the time to bring home his paycheck, when he had one." I remembered, but I wanted to hear it again. "I was making more money than he did by the time I was ten years old." He had a way of shaking his head whenever he talked about his dad, slow and looking in the distance. "I don't think the poverty bothered him any more than it bothered my mother. They just accepted it, just like everyone else. People in Laurinburg, North Carolina, paid twenty-two percent interest on their grocery bills at the company stores. When the doctors told my dad how much it would cost for them to treat my mother for blood poisoning, he just walked away."

I'd never seen a single picture of my dad when he was a kid, but I knew the details from all the stories, and I could see it all: the dirty mill village where he stole a bike and the front wheel came off at the bottom of Luce Hill; the tableful of brothers and sisters eating pintos and rice, night after night; his grandmother, the one everyone called Ma, who had to put her kids in the orphanage during the war because she couldn't afford to feed them; and my dad's mom, who before she died prayed so hard one night that the blood stood out on her forehead. My dad, even when he was kid, would have been so much bigger than anyone else, and his voice would be exactly the same, just as deep, still coming from everywhere at once. His hands would be rough, cut from all the hard work, his knuckles swollen from fistfights with kids who lived in the all-white sections of town, who called him retarded, who when they got older wore stiff white shirts and raced in cars their parents bought them. His hair grew wild and long because his mother was afraid of trimming it, afraid he would leave home, like he did, and leave her with the four younger children and no money to feed them. Whenever he told us this my stomach flinched.

He slept sometimes in the woods, to get away from the noise. He wore men's clothing, old and too big, but he made sure it was clean every morning, and he knew what clothes to look for at the Salvation Army, the ones the rich kids gave away. Even when he was a boy, I knew, he measured his voice the same way, listening to the sound of it like he was watching it in the mirror, so that it came from the pit of his chest right through the black of his eyes.

"When you got in fights did you ever get hurt?"

"Every goddamn time," he laughed. "I fought plenty, but listen. People can get killed, or maimed if you're not careful. This kid at school who's bugging you—"

I wanted him to talk, just not about Edgar. But there was no way to say anything.

"Lean in when you talk to him. That's all you got to do. Tell him you're afraid you're going to hurt him. Say it like you've got a knife he can't see. Just do it that way. You know, peaceful. Cause we might be around here for a while this time. And we don't need to make enemies unnecessarily.

"This house," he said, "You got to know what it means to your mother. I know she worries about it, about the money, about what it costs to get the right materials. But she'll see, when I'm finished, she'll understand." He swept one hand upwards. "It's all part of the plan," he said carefully. "By the time you're ready for college, I want those people to know, you come from a place where the finer things are appreciated. You can't walk into a place like Harvard University if they think you're just another smartass sharecropper's kid."

He would talk about important things now; it was almost like just saying the word Harvard was enough. "I've lived different lives," his voice boomed in the cab of the truck. I leaned my head against the window and let his sounds hum in me. He talked about his days in the Army, when he didn't socialize off base with the other enlisted men, he walked away when they griped, he did his work carefully, and he got to do what he'd left Laurinburg to do. He carried money in his pocket. He ate at decent restaurants where they treated him with dignity, not knowing who he was. He lived the way he'd seen officers live, as far from anything poor as he could afford, in a studio apartment. He wore pressed cotton shirts, had a pair of Florsheim shoes, and he spent time in museums.

Just before he went AWOL, he bought a set of paints. He told me about those few days, when he had so much to paint, how he let the wild shapes and brilliant colors loose on the canvas. "I'd gone to some museum somewhere and they had a van Gogh. You know who that is, don't you?" I nodded.

"Then you know, I'd just heard all about him and I saw that painting and I thought, shit, I'd cut my ear off too if I saw the goddamn world that screwed up."

At least I knew now what it meant that he went AWOL. I'd just read about it in a book about the Civil War, where they shot a guy for running off. Before that, I thought he was saying a wall, and that it just meant that he'd started building things, nailing studs and plates.

This time though I wanted to know what really happened. I asked him.

"About AWOL?" he said flatly. "I'll tell you." But he didn't, for a long time. He just drove, dark in the eyes, like I wasn't there.

"I'll tell you," he said finally, like the last ten minutes hadn't even happened, "there's stars and there's a thing called black holes. The black holes, you go in, and that's it. You don't go anywhere after that." He kept making loose fists and looking at them. I brushed some sawdust off my arm.

"Anyway," he said, "once we get settled, I believe I'll start doing some art again. Some sculpture, something real. Then again I might be just as happy cutting off an ear." He parked in front of the bank, but didn't get out of the truck. "I could start with this banker," he laughed. "I mean, what in the hell does a banker need two ears for?"

In the bank, Mr. Randolph shook our hands. His hands were white and soft. He was pale, but not thin, with a picture of his family on his desk. I could smell the outside still in our clothes.

"This is my son," my dad said. Curls of his black hair stood from his head like little black flames. "He's a smart kid. I thought he might learn a thing or two while we knocked out this loan agreement."

Mr. Randolph smiled. "Well," he said, not hurrying, "you come right along. And if you have any questions, let me know." He turned to my dad. "We've got all the papers already here, pretty much routine. Of course, if you have any questions, anything at all, we'll work it out." Another man sat waiting in a little conference room. He looked at his watch, and smiled at us. He was big, and he spoke so suddenly and so loudly that I caught myself before I could sit down. "You know," he laughed to my dad, "I could have sold that land a dozen times since I took your offer. You got yourself a hell of a deal, there, Everest Revel. But, what the hell." He regarded me. "Excuse my French." He spread his round, meaty hands out on the table, his rings glittering in the light.

My dad didn't say anything. The armchair he sat in was not small, but it hardly seemed able to hold him.

The man laughed again. "I tell you, though, Mr. Revel, you're all right in my book. You ever think about getting in the spec house business, we could probably make some good money. I've got another couple of parcels on the south side. Might be a little gold mine. Any hoo—so, this your lawyer?" He made a pistol with his white hand and clicked it at me. "Got that look in his eye. Sharp."

I hadn't realized I was looking at him so closely. It was his voice, his words had a way of floating. I turned away. It started when I turned my head—I let it rock a little, it made everything in the room so suddenly quiet and easy. Then I caught my dad's glare out of the corner of my eye. I held my head still.

Mr. Randolph took out a packet of papers. "Here's what we've got, gentlemen," he said, and started passing pages out to my dad. "Everything here's pretty standard stuff, payment schedule, construction draw schedule, mortgage insurance, survey, title search," he went on, laying documents down with each item. I glanced at them, and at my dad. He drummed his heavy fingers on the table, not looking at me, or at the papers. There were so many words falling in front of him I wondered how long it would take us to read all of them. I'd seen my dad reading a few times before, moving his finger deliberately under each word, mouthing each word, his whole face straining to get through a few lines. I pulled one of the pages out of the stack to skim one of the paragraphs. In the first sentence I could already see how lost I was: I had no idea what they meant by guarantors and premium coverages, I couldn't even figure out how they were numbering the pages.

"Careful there, son," Mr. Randolph said pleasantly, "we got to kind of keep these things in order, you know."

He hadn't finished handing the pages out when my dad spoke. He wasn't shouting, but still I could feel his words through my fingers on the table. "This is all fine," he said. A steel flashed in his eyes, and his hand lay on the papers. Mr. Randolph stopped, his eyes suddenly weak behind his glasses. The other man raised his eyebrows, not smiling. My dad went on. "I expect everyone here knows what we're agreeing to. I expect we'll all live up to what we said we'd do."

He had gone right to the soft place in those two men, like he had a gun aimed at them under the table. It scared the breath out of me at first. I peeked at Mr. Randolph's ear, even though I knew my dad had meant it as a joke. I thought for just a second that my dad would throw the papers, or even turn the huge conference table over on them. Even when he didn't do any of that, when he just let some of his anger soak silently into the walls around us, I knew that the peculiar stillness of the air between the men in that room was a dangerous thing, a thing all of them recognized. Mr. Randolph tried to laugh, but it came out too softly. "Sure, just like we said, Mr. Revel. It's a twenty-year land contract on the land, and a thirty-year construction loan on the house. Both at ten and a quarter percent, with ten percent down."

"This boy," my dad put his hand on my shoulder, resting it almost too heavily for me to stay sitting straight, "is why we're here. I don't give a goddamn about all the quarter percents and wherefores and all that shit. I'm building a home for my family. This boy's got the brains to go to Harvard University, and I'm not going to let anybody or any money stand in his way. And I'm going to see to it that he lives in the kind of place Harvard students live."

I shivered, some with awe, but some with fear, that he was saying too much now. The men looked nervously to each other. "Okay, Mr. Revel," Mr. Randolph said, folding his pale hands together. "That's, you know, that's all fine, I'm sure. He sure looks like a bright kid," and he tried to laugh a little again, but it got caught. "We hope, you know, that the bank can, that's what we believe, you know, in helping people, even with some credit inconsistencies, to build..." He did then what I didn't expect, which was to look my dad square in the eye. "These are only details. But they're important details. We're talking about a lot of money here, and it's not strictly an owner financing arrangement. Take the draw schedule, for instance..."

"I follow you, Mr. Revel," the man with all the rings said. "I got no problem at all with what you're saying. I like that, I like a man who's not afraid to lay it on the line. I'll tell you, in my business, I get so goddamn sick of this paperwork bullshit myself, you know? A man's handshake, that should mean something."

Mr. Randolph was actually squirming now. "Gentlemen," he said, "do we want to move forward with this loan? I mean, I can't help all the," he waved his hands out nervously to the papers on the table, "all the papers. These are just the normal, the usual documents. Everyone signs exactly these same things."

The man with the rings laughed now, easily. "Sure, we understand," he said, nodding to my dad, "don't worry too much there. A bank's gotta do what a bank's gotta do. We'll get it all signed up pretty, no problem. I'm just saying, what Mr. Revel brings up here's a good point, you know. It's looking a deal in the eye is how you know if you really got a deal, not pussyfooting around with a bunch of legal mumbo jumbo." He was rubbing his hands together as he spoke. He turned to Mr. Randolph. "Let's get this shit signed and get out of here," he said. "I got my land up as collateral, the deed stays in trust. You got a no-lose situation, so let's work with Mr. Revel here. Got it?"

I had thought until then that Mr. Randolph, the banker, was the guy in charge. But now it was the guy with the rings who seemed to be telling everyone what to do. My dad had his fists closed and when he talked, he talked over their heads. I started to worry again that he would start yelling or turning over furniture.

But he hadn't moved his head, not even to look at the other men while they were speaking. "I'll tell you what," he said flatly. "Me and my boy are going to take a quick look at all this," and he pushed the pile of papers across the table to me. "That's good enough for me. And I'll tell you why. Like I said, because I don't care what you got written down. As long as we all understand, I'm building the house I showed you on the land I walked off with Tom Prevatte here, and I'm paying what you told me I'd be paying for it every month, as long as we understand that, we're set."

The men nodded slowly. After a while, Mr. Randolph

started talking again, very quietly, saying every time before he started, "and I'm required by law to explain," or "we're required to disclose, for your protection." He mentioned the draw schedule a couple of more times. My dad listened like a stone, training his eyes to a dead place between the men. I began leafing through the pages. My fingers grew colder and colder around the stack. I wished I could whisper to my dad to ask what I should look for, but I knew better. Every sentence knotted up in figures and legal words. Some of the sentences were so long that even if I read them twice I could not understand what they were about. The columns of numbers were not for adding or multiplying, but seemed to begin and end without reason. Everywhere I saw dollar amounts and percentages, but there was nowhere that it said how much we would owe, or have to pay. After a while, whenever I tried to fasten on even a word it swam straight to my stomach. I saw one picture, marked *survey*, that was something like a blueprint except I didn't understand anything except the lines. I tried passing some of the pages over to him to read, but he just held them up without moving his eyes at all.

I didn't know that the room was quiet until my dad reached over and pulled back the stack of papers, even the one I was holding, without a word. He began slowly printing his name on page after page, writing out each letter like he had to think about it. I almost stopped him when he got to the pages I hadn't read yet, but I could see not to. The man with the rings nodded and smiled to me, like he was saying it was all right. Mr. Randolph's face was white, and shiny wet even though I couldn't see any sweat. When it was all over and we stood up to leave, Mr. Randolph's hand jumped a little—I think he wanted to shake on the deal, but we didn't. We just left both of them standing in the room, like we'd actually shot them.

Mrs. Winthrop's Flowers

CARSON WAS RIGHT—one afternoon when I was home by myself I looked in my mom's closet. I opened the suitcase, and there it all was—a brand new toothbrush and tube of toothpaste, some clothes, the stuff she'd need to go away. I even found a hundred and fifty dollars and some blank checks in a pocket in the side of the suitcase.

I'd read a story once in school about a boy who carried a small, blurry photograph of his mother all the time. She had left when he was three. At night the boy put it beside his pillow, sometimes dreaming that he felt her hand on his forehead just before he awoke. He even brought the picture with him to college, taped it in a book where he looked at it only once in a while, until he stopped feeling her hand at all. When the boy was older, with his own children in college, he found the book again by accident and saw the picture of his mother. He remembered how many nights he had felt that quiet hand, he remembered right where her fingertips lay on his eyebrows and how she moved his hair. He cried like he did when he carried the picture every day, only worse because there was no hand and there was no mother, and what he had waited for in his sleep all those years was nothing but a blur, eyes that were no more than dark dots, a dress shaped the only way he ever figured a mother could be shaped, just light and shadows on a piece of paper that he could tear apart as easily as he could turn a page.

I closed my mom's suitcase, but I didn't leave the closet. My dad's Carhartt coat hung on a nail. I started to reach into the pocket of it, but I was too scared. I saw a pack of cigarettes up on a shelf and I thought about sneaking one. I didn't do that either. Next to the cigarettes, behind a balled-up sweater, I saw the corner of an old shoebox, one I'd seen a long time ago somewhere, with a bunch of rubber bands around it. Even though I wanted to open the box, I was afraid to. My blood was speeding up. When I reached my hand to touch the box, to see if I dared, my hand went strangely white and was so cold I could hardly feel the cardboard. I couldn't hear anything now, no birds, no cars, nothing but my blood. I took the box down but not out of the closet. I set it on my mom's suitcase and pulled at one of the rubber bands. I'd never actually been told not to go into their closet—in fact, a couple of times my mom had asked me to go in and get something. And they'd never said anything about the shoebox, either—it wasn't like her purse—I knew she didn't like me in there—but then again, I did know, because of where it was, and how it was pretty much hidden, that I wasn't supposed to do it.

Mostly it was boring. I did see my own birth certificate, which I'd never seen, and that made me think about how I used to ride on my dad's shoulders, at least we had a picture

of me on his shoulders. I found his discharge—honorable—
from the Army. There was another piece of paper stapled to it
that said some things about a court-martial, and that the
verdict and sentence were classified.

I read it one more time and then I folded it exactly like it
had been, put the bands around the box, put it all back, and
walked outside. It didn't really bother me that people like the
guys in the bank might be a little afraid of my dad—it almost
made him seem like he had some kind of special power. And
the way he'd talked about the fights he'd gotten into growing
up in North Carolina, people were right to carry some respect
for him. A court-martial made sense, but I hadn't seen
anything about him having to go to prison. And it would
make sense for me to ask him about that. I'd just have to wait
for the right time, like when we'd go somewhere for a cup of
coffee, and I could say something simple like *What did they say
when you came back after you were AWOL?* Or I could say
something to my mom, I could probably even just ask her, *Did
Dad ever have to go to jail after he was AWOL?* Those things would
make sense to say.

I wrapped the box as carefully as I could then went out to
the dining room, where we had a photo album. I didn't even
think about it, I just took a picture of me and Carson from the
summer we lived in Maine. When we moved we got all new
moving boxes. The picture showed us standing inside one. I
went back to the closet and put the picture in the pocket of my
mom's suitcase.

Even after I'd seen the suitcase, I knew my mom wouldn't
really leave. We had a contract for the house now, and lots of
money—thousands of dollars from the bank. I was sorry she
worried the way she did, but if she'd seen him in the bank,
she'd know—he would never let anyone do anything to hurt

his family. Just like when he'd let me steer his truck, years ago, I knew he wouldn't let me drive into a tree. Besides, we'd already moved so many times—where would she go that she hadn't already been?

When we first moved to Michigan, I'd started going to Gethsemane Lutheran Church because it didn't look like any church I'd ever seen. The building, outside and inside, was all made of the same, plain concrete, of what looked like a single wall that rose and fell, never coming to a corner. The windows were cut in at deep angles, and the stained glass was not of any pictures, only designs. The floor was polished concrete, with red carpet runners. Even the altar was made of concrete, an impossible shape that came to a point at the bottom, balanced just so. Whenever it was touched I caught my breath.

When they began the worship, the organ sounded from every inch of those concrete walls. Then came the crucifer, acolytes, worship assistants, all in white, then the choir, in robes of blue and green and red and yellow, their voices swelling and falling, and finally the pastors, in robes stitched with crosses and fish and fires. When we spoke or chanted together, our voices echoed, slightly, just enough to stick. When we quit singing and the music quit playing, the silence came so suddenly that I always waited for the walls to fall in on us.

They posted the scripture lessons weeks ahead of time. The Sunday they were going to read my favorite Bible passage, I asked if I could go up to the pulpit to read it. I'd thought maybe, since I'd quit my sermons from trees and roofs, I might try actually talking in front of real people. At first the pastor shook his head, like he'd say *Kids don't do that*, but then he turned, like he was listening for something.

"You've got to say exactly what's printed," he said. "Just don't get up there and do anything original."

Now, when I stood at the pulpit, my voice came back to me so small and high from the walls that I stumbled after only a few words. And when I raised my eyes for the first time I really did see a throng of people, a massive churchload of them, and I faltered again, but only for a moment. Then the words came out from deep in my body, and it felt good.

"You are God's fellow workers," I read, wishing I could raise my arms, "you are God's field, God's building. As a wise master builder, I laid a foundation, and another is building upon it. But let each man be careful how he builds upon it. For no man can lay a foundation other than the one which is laid, which is Jesus Christ." I paused. My skin pulled tight, and dampness set in. When I looked to the passage again, I couldn't find where I'd left off. I closed my eyes, looked to the sea of faces, and I read the rest of it, almost without looking at the page again. "Now if any man builds upon the foundation with gold, silver, precious stones, wood, hay, straw, each man's work will become evident; for the day will show it, because it is to be revealed with fire." The words sang through me. I could see the fire devouring the straw, I could hear the flames wanting more. "And the fire itself will test the quality of each man's work." The reading was supposed to go on but I closed the book. They waited. I went back to my seat.

"That was beautiful. How you read that." The woman beside me whispered through a fog of dead air. I didn't know her. She was young, not young like a kid, but like Frankie. When she turned her head I could smell flowers. Her dress was silver with gold flowers stitched to it. "Talk to me after church," she said. She touched her fingertips to my arm.

My heart pounded so loud, I knew she could hear it. I

didn't know whether to turn to her or not. She still had her fingertips to my arm, and her voice was coming to me now through my skin. Finally I found her eyes; they were wet at the edges.

"Okay," I said, and the choir stood, and the music rained from the rafters. For the rest of the service she moved in small ways that kept catching the light in the gold and silver of her dress. She did not touch me again. All the sounds of the church—the coughs, the bulletins rustling, the pastor's steady voice, and the voices around me—all got smaller and smaller. I tried to follow along, but over and over I felt her fingertips, in the same place, going deeper and deeper, even though she didn't touch me. Her flowers took over more and more of the air, mixing with the grownup smell of her skin, the traces of coffee and cigarettes. I did not think of her skin, I would not do that, but my own skin, under my clothes, itched horribly for me to move, to make my clothes brush against it. When the service ended and the parade of robes went past, she stood up. I stood, too, my muscles unfreezing, the numb needles under my clothes draining my memory. Had I gone up for communion? Had I stood during the Lord's Prayer with everyone else?

She put her hand to my shoulder when we walked from the sanctuary. Her touch went straight to my knees. We left out a side door, bypassing the line going to the pastor, down a hallway where a few other people were gathering, talking, dividing up, down another hallway, empty but for us, into one of the Sunday School rooms. She still had my shoulder. The room smelled like little kids, like their crayons and paste. She let go when we sat in the little chairs.

"Well," she said, "I know your mom or dad is probably ready to get home."

"Um," I faltered. "Well, they're not here. I just come by myself."

She picked up my hand from my lap. "You really read that with heart," she patted her own heart. My breath came in hummingbird beats. My hand was numb in hers. "I think this must be a very special church to have someone like you."

She let go of my hand. "I have a son your age." She breathed sharply. The smell of her flowers was getting heavier. Her voice caught. "Oh, how do I say this? You know, I came to this church today. I haven't been to a church, I guess, since I got married. I'm not really a church kind of person. Maybe I should have been. Maybe then—" The edges of her eyes filled, but she didn't wipe them. "I don't know what I came here for. I just don't know what to do with him anymore. He's a good boy, I know he is. But some of these boys he goes around with, I think that's a big part of what's wrong. If I could just get him around kids like—like you."

I remembered what Carson had said, that I needed a friend. "What's wrong with him?"

"Nothing, nothing at all. They act like he's some kind of demon or something, but he is a good boy. I just can't control him anymore." She looked around at the little kids' pictures on the walls. "Chris needs someplace like this, I can tell you that."

The way she said his name, I imagined a kid with those starving television eyes, stranded out in some cold, remote run-down house, all alone except for a few boys at school who only bothered with him enough to get him to take the blame for their trouble. There would be something smart about him, for sure—some way he had of reading books too close, of letting them get lost inside his head—but he'd also be the kind of kid his teachers wouldn't understand. And here was his own mother, saying she thought I could save him somehow.

More Like Not Running Away

"My name's Julia," she said. "Julia Winthrop. But you can call me Julia." She told me that her son had been caught setting fires in the woods behind their apartment, because one of the fires went out of control, burning almost a half acre of underbrush. "He and these boys, they sneak out at night. At midnight! What am I supposed to do, put locks on his window? I don't know what else they get into." She sounded worried, but a little curious too. "Anyway, it's been so long since he's had a friend, a real friend that's not just dragging him into places he needn't be." She patted my knee.

The part about the fires, that didn't sound good. On the other hand, I thought, what if I could actually be the person to get this kid back from the edge before he burned down somebody's house—he might even kill someone someday, unless he got help. But what would I say? *Hey, you know, matches are dangerous? Your mom wants me to be your friend?* And what if he was like all the other kids I knew, just talking about baseball, or girls, or calling guys queer?

"You know, Mrs. Winthrop," I said.

"You can call me Julia," she said.

"I don't know too much about the other kids here. I mean, if you did bring him, it seems like for some people who come here, things just get worse."

"What makes you say that?" She looked very lost now and I felt sorry for her, because here she'd come to me like I had some kind of answer for her kid who liked to burn things and now I was basically saying that it would almost be worse if he came to church. I was pretty surprised I would even say it, and it got me to realize how much nothing I'd been hearing sounded like God anymore.

"I don't mean there's anything wrong with this church. I don't think that's what I mean. It just seems like a lot of the kids who come here don't really want to. I think their parents make them. Like my dad, he says you start thinking God's on your side. He told me once that the last place somebody needs God is in church."

"He doesn't come here, does he?"

"My dad? No."

"Why do you? I mean, if you don't think it helps?"

I'd known she would ask that but it still wasn't any easier to answer. I saw the pictures of lambs and crosses on the wall. "I used to think, I thought I heard—"

"God." She said it like she'd known all along.

I nodded. Whenever somebody found out about the things I heard, they acted worried. I'd stopped saying anything about it a long time ago, even before we'd moved to Colorado when I was eight, but some people found out anyway. Like my math teacher, I remember—she'd pulled me aside one day and said she thought something was wrong, because of how I covered my ears so much. I tried to stop after that, but it kept happening.

"Maybe you really did hear God," she said. "I've heard of that. Just as long as he's not telling you to hurt anybody."

I shook my head. "I used to think I knew what he was saying, but now it all comes out mixed up, and in different voices." I hadn't realized my head was still nodding until she reached over and steadied my chin.

"I don't know anything about your dad," she said, "but don't hold it against him if he doesn't come." She turned away from me for a second. "I should have done things different, so different, I know. I see Chris now and I know, he doesn't hear me anymore."

"What did you do when you found out about him starting those fires?"

She smiled, but not really. "I tried to ask him why. I guess that's what I really wanted to know, why he'd do something so awful. I said, 'Did you think about the little animals that probably got burned up when you did that?' I asked him if he'd considered the possibility he might have burned down someone's house, maybe even killed somebody. And he'd have to live with that the rest of his life." She pulled a pack of cigarettes from her purse, a long, skinny pack. Then she looked around and let out a little laugh, like she might cry. "I almost asked if I could smoke in here," she said, laughing again. "Guess I've been going on."

I could see a house burning and a kid's face pressed to the window, trying to breathe. "Mrs. Winthrop," I said, "if he did do that, I mean, and I know it would be a really terrible thing, but if you didn't know, if there was a fire and you didn't know he'd done it, but you thought maybe he did, would you want him to tell you? Even if it meant something bad would happen to him because of it?"

"Of course," she said. "Of course. I love him. I'd love him even if he killed somebody. Isn't that what you're supposed to do?" She stood up and went to the door. "I've got to have a cigarette," she said. "Isn't that awful? I've just got to have one. I did get through that whole church service, though, and that's something, isn't it?"

When we went out she lit a cigarette. "I can't believe I just had a conversation like that with someone your age. I hope it's okay. I mean, I hope I didn't lay too much on you there."

I didn't know what she meant. Her cigarette smelled of flowers just like she did. I thought just then to ask her how she did find out about things that Chris did wrong, about the fires, and what she'd say to him if he ever did really hurt somebody, but by then we were talking about other things, the things people always talked about, school and weather, and then it was like we'd never talked at all.

I went to the church a few more times, and I always looked for her or her son, but I never did see either of them. I had a thought after that, a thought like being hungry but not knowing what to eat, about starting a fire myself because I wanted for my mom to say something to me the way Mrs. Winthrop talked about Chris, for my mom to be a little afraid for me. I did take some matches one day and lit a small pile of straw on fire, but it burned out. I don't know if I was afraid of getting caught, or of really hurting someone or something, or if I just wanted to see it burn itself out, but that was all I did. I buried the ashes, though, so there wasn't really any way for my mom to find out.

I knew that people didn't really go to Hell for doing things like that, but I did think about it. I even touched the hot match head to my finger. I never heard if Jesus was lonesome in Hell, but it would be hard to live in a place like that knowing it was full of people who hated him—so much that they'd tried to kill him. It was so sad that people cried for him for hundreds and hundreds of years, long after anyone could remember the color of his hair or the exact shape of his face.

I had done a terrible thing, though, in telling Mrs. Winthrop that a church might not be the best place to take her son. But I think she actually kind of liked that he was in trouble. It must have worried her, especially the fires—I'm sure it did—but I think she must have looked around that church and seen something that worried her even more.

The Right Words to Somebody

ABOUT A WEEK LATER EDGAR SURFACE came up to me at lunch and started nodding his head back and forth. "Oh man," he moaned, "I feel it, baby. I feel it." Some kids laughed and he smiled with his teeth. He put out his hand like he was going to flick me but he didn't, he kept stopping just short, flicking the air. Then he nodded, flipping his hair.

I hit him between the eyes so hard that he went down without a sound. In an instant he was up again, taking wild swings. Nothing came close to me; I had all the time I wanted to duck, to hit him again. A silence wrapped around us, slow, slow, like I could hit him forever. I landed one directly on his nose and that was it. The kids around us gasped, then some teachers were there, holding us. I was amazed that Edgar was actually crying, in the hallway, on the way to the principal's office. I wondered if I was crying too. I reached my hand to my cheek but it was dry.

More Like Not Running Away

When I first hit him, it was so quiet at first, all the noise was caught inside me—the kids, the teachers talking to us, the dull, wordless voice of the principal, and through it all, my dad. He wasn't there, of course, and at first I actually thought it was God again, but I knew better, and I recognized it was my dad right after I hit Edgar. My dad wasn't saying anything in particular, just familiar words like he said at the table, like he was saying it right behind my head, like—like I was sitting in his lap the whole time, like we were driving that truck across the field again, and I was steering. Calm. So calm, it scared me worse than the actual fight.

My mom didn't ask about my cuts or bruises; she put her hand to my forehead the next morning and said, *Well, fever or no, you're staying home anyway.* They'd sent a note home. I never read it, but for some reason I didn't think I was really in much trouble.

"You finally get in a fight?" my dad asked. He was filling his Thermos with coffee.

I didn't answer.

"I'll tell you what's the matter," my mom said, "it's like a factory. Everybody's got to fit just so, got to stay just inside the lines."

"Well," my dad said, putting his hand very gently to my shoulder, "if you're going to be a tough guy, you might want to carry a first-aid kit with you. You never know when you're going to hit somebody too hard in the nose, you might have to put a tourniquet around their neck to keep him from bleeding to death."

My mom couldn't help laughing. "Well, I think what he really needs is a break," she said. She was a believer in staying home from school. We drank coffee all morning, then she broiled lamb chops for lunch, and we gnawed the bones. She pulled out the blueprints and traced her finger along the walls so seriously, lightly penciling in places where she had questions. "These windows," she asked, "are they standard sizes, so I can just buy drapes at the store? How much extra is this fireplace in the dining room? Because, you know, I'm not really sure we need it." She inspected every line of the materials estimates, asking me about items she didn't recognize, comparing prices on doorknobs and shoe molding. She shook her head at the totals. I was surprised at how many answers I knew; after all the days of tagging along with my dad to jobsites, of listening to the run-on conversations with subcontractors and superintendents, I'd absorbed more then I knew. I told her about linear feet, yards of concrete, rough openings, and overhangs.

Afterwards we walked three miles to the gas station to pick up our car. It was cold, and a few lazy snowflakes fell on us. "Your dad tries so hard," she said as we walked, "he wants us to have a place. He knows how other kids can be. He always worries that they won't leave you alone."

"They leave me alone. They're not bothering me."

She nodded. "It was hard when you were born. He was halfway across the country, still trying to sort things out from his trouble with the Army. And they put me to sleep, you know. I always felt bad about that, that you were born and there wasn't anyone there to hold you."

The snow landed on the places where my face hurt. I liked it. "They had a bulldozer at the land yesterday," I said.

"Well, your dad's always been one for the big production." She loved this. It was one of the things about him that she acted like was a problem at first, but always, the more she talked, the more she couldn't hide it: she was an admirer of dreams, of grand gestures, of mystery. Anywhere on earth, she'd say, people would recognize his genius—if he ever stopped in one place long enough for them to find out. "He thought I was some kind of movie star. I knew it the minute he came up to me, I was the star and he was the director. Some movie it turned out to be, huh?"

The way my dad told the story, it was the way she smoked. The first time he ever saw her, she was playing games with the cigarette. "I'd seen it a dozen times," he'd told me, "some kid just like her there at the Mission Inn in California, pretending to be famous. They all smoked the same way, like they thought movie stars smoked, and they all looked just like kids. What killed me was the way she tried to drink her Scotch." She had the drinking moves down, he always said, the glass loose in her hand. She had the lost money look, like a runaway Vanderbilt, mixed up with some city air, traveled air. She had the other men in the restaurant turned in their chairs, wondering at her lonesomeness, her thin dress, her untouched food. But when the Scotch hit her throat, all that fell apart in a fit of coughing and hiccups. She tried to dab the tears with her palm, but they were too much. When she tried to take a drag from her cigarette, more coughs, more hiccups, and then she was out the door. He followed her. She screamed at him. Just like a movie.

"I didn't want a thing to do with him," my mom said now. She held her cigarette so carelessly, so easily. "I wanted someone with some money. That's why I went to California in the first place. That, and to get away from all the same day after day at home. But then he had those eyes, that made me think. He has the kind of eyes that can make a woman ashamed of things she's never done."

She stubbed out her cigarette. "You're another one," she winked at me, just glancing at the cut over my eye. "Just be careful. People are likely to look at you and think you're more trouble than you are." Then she laughed. "Then again, maybe you are."

When we got to the gas station, the man behind the counter handed her the invoice. I could tell what she was going to do from how she held the paper, away from her.

"I think something's wrong." She folded the paper on the counter in front of the station manager.

He unfolded it. His mouth didn't look like it could close all the way. His eyes bulged slightly. "What do you want me to do? The price is what's on there." His greasy fingers tapped the counter.

"If you think that the single mother of four little children is going to stand by and let you terrorize her with these prices, think again." She lied so plainly, but there was a quiet, hard edge like my dad's.

"Ma'am," the manager said, "here's the price I paid for the parts. And here's how long it took to do it."

I tried to sit still in the hard plastic chair. There was a gumball machine next to me and I tugged absently at the lever.

"Just six months ago you told me these brakes were fine. I paid you thirty-five dollars for new pads. You think I don't know what you people do back in there?" She leveled a finger to the garage.

"They were fine six months ago. They get old." He still hadn't moved his head.

"Well I know a thing or two about getting old." She brushed the hair from her eyes. "Raising four kids on the money I've got. Save your 'extra charges' for one of these fat cats in the Cadillacs. Get out a pencil and refigure this. I'm not paying it. Not that much."

More Like Not Running Away

My mom's one great expertise was lying. She never told big lies, as far as I knew, but she loved to play a part. It was one consolation to all the moving, she said, that she could be dying of bone cancer in one town and thinking about giving half a million dollars to the library in another, and before anyone could get to the truth of it, she'd be halfway across the country. A few times, when someone had managed to find out our new address or phone number, she'd started crying, louder and louder, saying how they'd arrested my dad for being in organized crime, and giving them a government number to call to collect what we'd owed. Then she'd change our phone number again, and Carson and I would learn a new one all over again.

Reluctantly, the manager fingered the invoice. "See here, ma'am," he said, scratching his beard like it hurt, "this is the price of the parts. I call the parts store, and I write the price right on the invoice. That's what we pay."

"And what's this?"

"That's our labor. Four hours. And that's what it took."

She shook her head. "Now really," she said. "Four hours? I could have done it myself in less than that."

I could see then that the manager was giving up. If it was my dad, he'd of stared a hole in the guy, but not my mom. She had him in her eyes too, but he wanted to be there. I asked my dad once why he just stood there when she was screaming at him, why he didn't just slam the door and leave until she shut up. "Can't you see it," he'd said, "haven't you watched her when she does that, how her lips can't make the words she wants to say? That's who she is. She's so beautiful then, everything's right at the edge of her skin." Right now she was a skyscraper with fire in the windows, and the manager held up his hands.

He knocked thirty dollars off the price.

"That's more like it," she said. "I knew something was wrong. Maybe next time I come here"—the manager breathed in now through his tight lips—"we won't have to go through this." She winked, and came over to me at the gumball machine. "You don't need that," she said, "let's go." I could smell the Jergen's lotion on her hands, her makeup, her shampoo. We went to the car, and she gripped the steering wheel with both hands, until the bone white of her knuckles made them look as hard as my dad's. For a while we drove in silence, the icy wind through her window sweeping a wild part in her hair. I reached over and put my hand under hers on the seat. She wrapped her fingers around it, and I slid closer.

"Four kids?" I said.

She laughed like she'd been holding it in. "I just couldn't say a dozen, not today," she said. "Besides, where would I put any more than four? That's all we need, for your dad to get in his head that we need an even bigger house. To tell you the truth, though, money's tight," she said. "Your dad had a raise coming, but it didn't work out, there were tests he had to take that he didn't know about. So we can't be spending money we don't have on repairs."

She waved the invoice at me. "Get me a cigarette, will you, honey?" I reached in her purse and pulled out one of her slender cigarettes. They smelled softer than my dad's. He didn't like how she always tried different brands.

"You want me to light it for you?"

"Sure." Without even turning her head, she pushed in the cigarette lighter. When it popped out, I lit the cigarette. I'd never liked the taste before, but today I did. When she took it, the smoke rose in jagged streams.

"Mom, why did he run away?"

More Like Not Running Away

"You mean from the Army?" She slowed down a bit. "Well, you know he'd had all kinds of trouble back home. You know, fights—the bad kind, I mean, the kind where someone really gets hurt—and trouble with cars, with the police—"

"Like when he went to Myrtle Beach with those guys that time, and drove the car on the pier, right?" It was a story he'd told a few times at the table. "And when they rolled up some guy's finger in the car window—the guy who'd said something about Dad's sister—and they started driving."

She nodded her head, "Well, in a way. But this time he was in the Army. And he knew, if they caught him, they'd—"

"Put him in jail?" I asked it easy, like I knew what she'd say. She didn't answer though.

Finally, she talked again, but it was like she wasn't talking to me. "Bad enough that he didn't think they'd care what he had to say about it, they'd say it was his fault, and in a way—"

I waited, hoping she'd say more.

She sped up. "I'm trying to tell you," she said. "You have to listen. He lost his temper. That's it. I'm not saying you have to go around worried about this all the time. He knows he's got to watch his temper. He hurt someone, and right or wrong, he didn't think the Army would hear his side of the story. So he left, and when he met me, he told me, he wouldn't get married until he'd cleared up this trouble, except—" she stopped. "I got pregnant, with you, and he decided right then and there to face the music. And he did. And he knew, and I knew, if the Army wanted, they could really make him pay—"

She turned to me. "And in fact," she said, "in fact, listen. This is really a new start for him. I think for the first time in his life he's trying to fit in. He's always run away. Even when he didn't have something to run away from, I think he was running away from what might happen, or what he might do.

Now he's seeing, he might have something worth hanging around for."

When we got to the land, this lost-looking snow covered the rocks, the trees we'd cut down, the brown, bent grass. A bulldozer had pushed up a few piles of smaller trees and brush into a mass of torn limbs and root balls. The dirt smelled naked and it made me shiver.

My mom kept shaking her head. "It's amazing when you think about it," she said quietly, "that there's really going to be a house here someday. Do you think," she caught her breath, "do you really believe it?"

"I guess I do."

"It takes money." She said it so softly, I almost missed it. She didn't even move her lips.

"You should have seen it at the bank," I said. "It was cool."

She put her hand to the cut over my eye. We were both getting cold, just enough that we were moving in trances. "You just don't know," she said, "it means so much to him that you're there with him. That you're helping."

A man in overalls came around from behind one of the piles of trees. He was carrying a red gas can, sloshing gas over the trees. He went along to the next pile, then walked away, set the gas can down, came back to the pile, and lit the match. My mom grabbed my arm. "Oh my God," she gasped. The flames crept so slowly—then in an instant the fire went impossibly high. The air cracked, filled with smoke, hot even to where we were standing.

"He's just burning the dead stuff," I said. "That's how they get rid of the trash."

"It's so exciting," she said, looking along the clouds of smoke. We watched a while—I don't know how long—jolting now and then when the fire popped, lost in the white glow inside the piles, tasting the cold ashes. Snow still fell. I wished the man in the overalls would go away. I wished there was a way we could lie on the bare ground near the fire and let the tiny snowflakes cover us.

"Levi," she said, "what happened to you at school? I mean, don't get me wrong, there's nothing wrong with a fight now and then, but is something else wrong? You've been—" she made a small nod with her head. Her hands were in her coat pockets now, her face red at the edges from the cold. I wished I could help her, the way she worried about my dad, and her little lies.

"I'm just excited about the house."

"Oh," she said. There was something else she wanted to say, but she didn't. I could hear the words catching in her throat.

My Aunt Frankie said once that my mom's mom had lost her mind. I knew what that meant. One day they came home from school and found her singing "I saw miles and miles of Texas" at the top of her lungs. She sang it over and over, until her voice was so weak that for two months after that she couldn't speak a word. They put her in a hospital; that's where she learned how to paint. We had some of her paintings, windmills and farmhouses, but they didn't look like anything a crazy person would paint. All the colors were just like they were supposed to be, all the shapes were just right, even her name at the bottom of the paintings was in neat block letters. All that happened before I was born. The only thing at all strange about her now was that when she sat next to me, she patted my hand almost constantly.

I wound up staying home from school for more than just that day. The next day I really was sick, with spikes of fever.

That night, and nights after that, I was locked into dreams, more awake than asleep. I went back to school after a few days, but I could hardly bring myself to sit up. Pleasant shivers would start if anyone touched me, even accidentally, shivers that soon turned hard and took my strength. I couldn't lift my eyes. People could hear my breathing. I could feel in my skin what they were thinking.

I began to think that I wasn't sick after all, that it was only my skin changing. Before, I'd heard everything with my ears. Some things I knew I wasn't meant to hear, like my parents through my bedroom walls, like my teachers talking about me when they went home, like my dad's voice at school, even when I knew he was at work. I still heard all this, but now I was hearing it in my skin too. I started to hold my arms close to my body, to curl up, even sitting in school, to make myself smaller so I didn't hear as much. When a kid next to me in class moved in his seat, his shirt scratching across his back, it scratched across my back too. When two girls huddled, like they always did, their hair in each other's faces, I had to brush my own face to stop the tickling. Even if I was alone, at night, the boards of the house pulling loose from the nails sent chills through my bed frame, right into my ribs.

"Why do you do that?" A boy in my class, I didn't know his name, stopped me in the hallway at school. He played basketball.

"What?" His face was a blur, eyes and hair and skin all melted together. He was kind of whispering, like he knew me.

"Shake your head like that. With your eyes kind of closed, like you're dreaming." He half closed his eyelids and rocked his head back and forth to show me. "Why do you do that?"

A small terror set in me when I saw what he was doing. I wanted to lean in, to pretend I had a knife. I made a fist.

"See? You're doing it now."

"I don't know," I said. The other kids from the school flowed around us like a swollen, noisy, wrecking river. I stopped my head.

He leaned closer. "Maybe you got narcolepsy," he said.

"What's that?" I wasn't sure if he was going to make a joke.

"This disease, where you fall asleep."

"How do you get it?" I checked around to make sure other kids weren't listening.

"Beats me," he said. "Some lady in my dad's office has it, though. He says she just checks out. Boom." He shut his eyes suddenly, then opened them.

"A girl in language arts likes you," he said. "She saw you fight that kid."

From the corner of my eye I saw his face, a real smile, with nothing behind it. Before I knew it, we were both smiling, and laughing, me and this kid I didn't know, saying words that didn't mean anything, the way all the other kids talked.

That night in the dark I couldn't remember what we said. I could hear our voices, I could remember the laughs, but the exact words were lost. They had to be important after all, I thought, they must have been exactly the right words, because I can never forget how they just rolled out.

He said someone liked me. I wished Carson had been there to hear him, how he said it. I would have told her, but I couldn't remember who he said it was. Maybe he didn't say.

My boss Duval talks with his hands. *He has this theory: never leave a bent nail, never put something in unless it fits exactly, even when it'll never show.* "Somebody's coming behind us," he'll say, "maybe fifty years from now, but either they're going to say good things or bad things." And he's right, we see the work, good and bad, that people fifty, a hundred years ago left us.

We were supposed to finish the steeple on this church today, but I broke a louver so now we've got to have one milled. Then we have to take the whole ventilation panel apart to put it in. I offered to pay, to do it myself, but he says no: "You'll learn more from making me pay for it than paying yourself." *Things never throw him, which I figure is good when we're always so high off the ground.*

I've worked two summers now with him, since I started going to Chapel Hill, and he's a talker but I like what he says. He's about thirty, with eyes like he's always about to laugh. He's got this dream of climbing Mount Everest, and he can't get over that my dad was named Everest. I tell him they have a climbing club at Chapel Hill. "Just use your own ropes," he says. "It costs, but it's worth it."

I love that part of our morning routine, checking our ropes. He's the most careful person I've ever known. We have all our tools on lanyards in case we drop them, but he gets concerned even about dropping a nail, because things get to be habits.

I ask him, if he does really climb Mount Everest, how he'll keep from getting lost. "You'll see," he says. *I'm not sure what he means, but he says that to me a lot,* "You'll see."

Watching the Tigers

CARSON CAME TO MY ROOM one day after school. "Look." She held up something made out of popsicle sticks and other stuff. "I made it in school today. It's the stable."

The stable my dad had been building was still only a floor; before he could finish, he'd had to start on the plans and loans for the new house. And now it was too late for sure. He'd poured the foundation and was framing walls.

An orange cat followed her into the room. She set the popsicle stable down on my bed and picked up the cat. Its belly was swollen. "It's Moses," she said. "I found her."

"What's the matter with him?"

Carson scowled. "You don't even know? She's pregnant. She's going to have kittens."

"It's a she? Why'd you name her Moses?"

Carson shrugged. "Mom said to."

"Because she wanders. I bet."

I picked up the stable. "You have to give the kittens away, you know."

"So. Moses doesn't care. As long as she gets to stay with us. That's what she wants."

"Beats forty years in the desert, I guess."

Carson rolled her eyes. "A kid in school said if their cat has kittens his mom just puts them in a bag and throws them in a lake." She sat next to me. "I bet you could finish the real stable. If you wanted."

I turned the model she'd made around in my hands. She'd woven twigs into the popsicle sticks, put aluminum foil along the roof, and even had cellophane windows. The doors were hinged with duct tape. "It's even got a place to put the hay in, see," she pointed to a square hole in one of the gables.

"It's really good," I said. "You should show it to Dad."

"What for? He'd just say, sure, we'll do that, and then he wouldn't. He doesn't care about Delilah."

"He does too."

The proportions of her stable were just right. Even the red and white watercolors looked real, almost old. "You could build it," she said. "You wouldn't even need him. You know all about that stuff. Mom says you do."

"I've got to help Dad on the new house."

She took the stable. "You know," she said, "Dad's the only one you ever care about, and he doesn't even do anything like other dads. He never plays catch with you, or takes you anyplace except for his work. Don't you ever wonder why he doesn't have any friends? He never does anything except talk. Like that's supposed to be so great."

I wished I had a way to show her, or explain to her, all the things about our dad she didn't know. He had plans. It wasn't just about a house. So what if he didn't watch football games and drink beer and take me out for milkshakes? He knew me better than that; he knew about places far away, so far none of us could even imagine them, and he was getting me ready to go.

Moses stretched her legs. Her kittens' hearts ticked, like they were under water.

"This girl likes me," I said. "In language arts. A kid told me."

"Who is it?" She didn't believe me.

I could see the kid again, the way he laughed, and I knew it really happened, but I wished I hadn't said anything to Carson. "I can't remember."

She picked up Moses. "Who cares," she said. "As long as it's somebody."

It seemed like we worked so many days at the new house, but it always looked the same, mostly holes and ditches in the ground. I tried to imagine if I had to build a whole church by myself some day, like Carson said, and what if I spent all my time building it but nobody would go inside? I wondered if I'd be there by myself then, just sinking and sinking, with a black anger like my dad's.

One Saturday morning my dad took me to Grand Rapids to pick up a day laborer to help him. The city hummed its own way, the traffic and shouting, even the hundreds of footsteps all caught up in drones and rolling waves. I loved the buildings. I loved not knowing what was inside so many of them. People lived and worked everywhere, thousands of voices buried behind thousands of walls. In all the places we'd lived, we'd never lived in a city at all that I could remember. We hardly even visited cities. I wanted to go inside, behind the signs, where the people were breathing, to run from the truck and look into the black painted factory windows, to open doors, to hear what they were saying deep inside the buildings.

"Wait here." We parked in front of the four-story stone Salvation Army building. I moved to the door, to ask if I could go in, but he was gone before I could put the question together. Inside the Salvation Army store, people wandered around tangles of lamps, sofas, and round racks each stuffed with clothes of one color—red shirts in front, even two whole racks of yellow pants. Little groups of people were talking to each other, picking at the clothes. I knew my dad had bought his clothes at the Salvation Army when he was a kid, but I couldn't imagine him in this store. He'd even stayed overnight in Salvation Army rooms when he ran away from home. He came out of the side of the building now talking to a man with dark, slick hair and soft wrinkles. The man's eyes stayed down, and he moved his feet carefully, like he wasn't sure the ground would stay still for him. When he got into the truck beside me, I could see the comb marks in his hair. His sweet, spicy smell made my tongue sticky.

"This is Mr. Duncan." My dad smiled like he knew him.

"Hello, son." The man's voice was warm.

We passed some apartment buildings, some with plywood over the windows. Kids were kicking at a bank of dark snow. "Do you live here?" I asked.

He paused like he knew the answer but forgot.

"Around here," he said. When he smiled, his mouth opened. His teeth were awful. His breath was getting sweeter, and I wished he'd roll down his window. "I been all over, though. Been up north, round Detroit some too. Don't much care for this winter though. Too cold, ain't it? He laughed like that was a joke. "You watch the Tigers any?"

It took me a second to put Detroit and tigers together. I'd never actually watched a baseball game. When the boys at school talked about it, they sounded like they were from a different country, talking about so many names and numbers and cities. And they always laughed when they talked about it, and pretended to fight. "Not really," I said.

"Don't know what you're missing, I got to say, kids and baseball is a natural. My old man, he played." He waved toward the city outside. "I don't mean on no team or nothing, just with me." He took a hungry breath. "You don't know what you're missing, kid, you should go see yourself a game sometime. Course, the Tigers ain't shit. Excuse me," he cut a worried glance to my dad, "but they ain't."

My dad looked a ways up the street. He didn't play any games, not cards, not even riddles. He even hated having too many questions in a row. Games were for people who didn't have enough real things to figure out.

When we got to the jobsite, my dad started telling Mr. Duncan to do something, saying it so gently that again, I wondered if he'd known him already. I walked around and picked up scrap lumber to throw in the burn barrel my dad had started. After a while, my dad called me over to the truck and poured us coffee out of his Thermos. Mr. Duncan kept working, slowly.

"He smells really nice," I said.

"Sweet," my dad said. "It's the wine."

"Is he drunk?"

"Not now. He'll finish up today, though, and drink a couple of bottles." My dad said it so matter of factly, like Mr. Duncan was going to write a poem.

"Is he married?"

"I doubt it, at least not anymore."

More Like Not Running Away

Mr. Duncan was stacking lumber in the distance. Even though I knew he wasn't married, and even though he was all by himself against the light snow, he didn't seem lonely.

"Can't somebody help him out? Give him a real job or something?"

My dad lit a cigarette. "Well, I'll tell you what. People probably have. Over and over. Some people, though, they're going to lose everything no matter what. It's what they do best, I guess."

"Why?"

"Feeling good scares them. They're always waiting for something to go wrong, so they make something go wrong, so they don't have to worry about it anymore." My dad's hands were red from the cold.

"Did you ever drink wine?"

"No. Getting drunk's the way people escape when what they really want is to get caught."

The white framing lumber, the walls and joists of the house, stood like a skeleton against the dark wall of trees.

"Can you see it?" My dad pointed to the house. I let my eyes haze, to blend the bare wood into a single finished shape, but I still couldn't make it out.

"Are those all the walls?"

He nodded. "And the ridge beams. I've still got to put in some blocking. Maybe when we get it sheeted, you'll see it better. I'll tell you one thing. It's sitting in exactly the right place. And facing the right direction. That's what I like best right now. That's the kind of thing you can't afford to screw up. I remember one contractor, putting up a tract house, got the foundation laid and damn near the whole house framed. On the wrong lot."

"No way. What did they do?"

"Tore it all down. Dug up the footings, even backfilled the holes. And you know what? Six months later, they put a house right there. Right where they'd just torn down three months of work. Just goes to show you."

I could see it, what he was talking about. If the house had been any higher, the treetops would have been hidden. And where the stream was, under one corner, made it look like the house was floating.

"Those prestressed concrete beams," he said, pointing to where the house went over the stream. "Jesus Christ, that damn near did us in."

"How'd you get them here?"

He shook his head. "They brought a tractor-trailer in here, if you can believe it, and had to use the dozer to get it back out. And we had to have a goddamn crane, which I'd figured we'd need, but God Almighty, we about could have bought one for what it cost to have it here for two days."

The longer I looked at the cantilever over the stream, the harder it was to believe that it would hold up so much of the house with nothing beneath it.

"You could drive a tractor out to the end of it," my dad said, "and it wouldn't bend an inch. And I'll tell you what's even more amazing. When it's done, you won't even see the beams. The siding goes right down the walls, right over the beams like they're not even there. I've even dropped the soffits down another foot, so the walls won't look any taller." He tried to show me with his hands how the roof and walls would meet differently.

Not many people can look at a stickframe house and be able to tell how it's going to end up; I never could until that day. It didn't take blurring my eyes, or even as much imagination as I'd have thought. It helped that my dad would hold his hand out to the house, pointing out the parts he was talking about, almost like he could put the pieces together with nothing more than his words and the weight of his gestures. And when I did get the picture, it wasn't like I'd thought it would be, like a photograph of something finished: what I saw, during that one easy afternoon with my dad, with my eyes closed, was the grass, under the snow, turned green and lifted up again, leading right to the front door.

That night he gave Mr. Duncan fifty dollars. We drove him almost all the way to the Salvation Army, but he said to let him out at a store on the corner. He got out, and we left, and my dad said that no matter how much some people wanted to do what was right, they mostly did what they had to do.

Day after day I helped on the house, after school, Saturdays, Sundays. I learned to balance loads of lumber on my shoulders, to think ahead of the tools my dad would need. I swung two-pound framing hammers dead straight. I could read level and plumb, balance easily on the three and a half inch wide perimeter walls to toenail the rafters, and even went to the second-story top plates with nothing between me and the ground.

One afternoon my dad laid a wormdrive Skilsaw on the plywood decking. He told me how he'd seen men lose their fingers, and why accidents were seldom accidents. People who thought they were in control forced a cut, binding the saw, or worse, relaxed, forgetting all the powers the saw had hidden in bowed lumber, knots, wet places. The guard over the blade on his saw was always tied open with a nail, so he could hold lumber with one hand and cut angles with the other. It was dangerous. It meant that the blade was exposed even before the saw hit the board. He told me these things with his voice going deeper and deeper, until he quit talking at all and I lost myself, only for a moment, in the silence.

Suddenly, the saw screamed out. He'd pulled the trigger and let the blade touch the plywood, so the saw flung back from him, high into the air. It came nowhere near me—in fact it went away, but still, the noise and the swinging of his arm scared me, and I hit the deck.

"I wanted you to see that," he said, setting the saw down. "When you pull this trigger, with the guard pinned up, the blade crawls right up your leg, right into your gut. It happens. You got to respect it."

He handed it to me, and told me to pull the trigger. My heart hadn't stopped pounding, but I did what he said to do. Even with my muscles so tight that my hand was white on the handle, when I pulled the trigger the sudden torque nearly twisted the saw from my hand. Then he took me to the side of the house, laid a two-by-four on the deck, with one end hanging over, and showed me how to hold it still by standing on it.

"It's heavy," he said, "made to cut down, so when you're framing you can drop it over and over, letting the weight do all the work, same reason we use the heavy hammers. I can tell if someone shows up for a job and says he knows how to frame, if he knows what he's doing. He pulls out some sixteen-ounce finish hammer, and I know right then, he's used to cutting on sawhorses and tinking nails. You might as well learn to use a real tool."

He showed me. He pulled the trigger and the saw ate through the wood like it was paper. I made a cut then, letting the saw sink like he did, amazed and breathless when I finished, still holding the handle too tight to let go even long after the blade stopped turning.

More Like Not Running Away

So I cut blocking; he called out the measurements and I marked two-by-fours, squared the lines, and fed the saw. At first my cuts had strayed so far from the lines that my dad couldn't use the blocks. He didn't say a word, he just called out the same measurements again. Eventually I learned not to push the saw at all, just set it as solid and true on the board as I could, then let it do the work. A few times I tried to make the cuts without squaring lines, just sighting it, the way I'd seen him do it, but it didn't work at all.

The first time the blade did bind up, when I'd started a cut just a hair off the mark and tried just to nudge the saw back on to the line, the saw came out of the two-by-four like a vicious animal, straight at me. The teeth stopped inches from my leg. I shook all the way to the truck, as afraid that my dad had seen it as I was of the blade. After that I knew what to anticipate, and when it bound again, I was ready for it, ready to keep it down.

We came home after eight o'clock, my clothes stiff with the cold and sawdust. I closed my eyes while my mom brought us dinner. We ate in silence, my ears still throbbing from the long hours of the whining saw, the drills, the hammering, and the drone of the generator.

"I can't believe it," my mom said. "It looks like a real house out there."

My dad set down his fork. "That back bedroom, I'm glad we decided on the cathedral ceiling. It makes the whole room."

"It's a miracle what you've been able to do," she said.

"The miracle is what we're building it for," he said. "There's not a damn thing standard about it." He looked around the dining room, at the discolored Kmart wallpaper. "It's ours. It's us." The calmness of his voice made my eyes heavy.

"Carson," my mom said, "why don't you show your dad what you made? You should see it."

Carson shook her head, but my mom nodded again. Carson left and came back with the stable and set it on the table next to my Dad. She opened the door for him to look inside.

"That's beautiful," he said, turning it and lowering his head to look inside. He nudged the door. One of the Popsicle stick braces came loose.

Carson picked it up and handed it to him. "That's okay," she said, "I can fix it." She pressed the stick back, but it didn't stay. "It's a stable." She waited.

"Oh, yes," my dad said, still so quiet and tired. "The stable." He looked to my mom. "We've got to have a place for Delilah here, don't we?" My mom nodded. "I'll tell you what," he said, "it won't take a day. I've got the worst of it done, and we're not at a bad place with the house."

"When do we get the next draw?" my mom asked.

"We'll get it soon enough," he said. "I'm not going to have it dried in over the garage yet, no point in that; it'll be close enough, though."

My mom put her hand to the back of my neck. "You have any homework to do?" she asked. I shook my head no. I did, but I knew I could do it after I went to bed. "He's so tired," she said, "we've got to be careful he can still keep up in school."

He looked at me across the table. "You'd be proud of him. He's working hard, doing a man's job. I couldn't do it without him."

That night I did as many algebra problems as I could before I fell asleep. I was behind in school, a little anyway, but I knew I could catch up. I had time on the bus, and in the morning. I had time.

More Like Not Running Away

That draw and another came through, even though, each time, the bank made some exceptions: we hadn't hung all the Sheetrock, and still hadn't insulated the attic—details, just like my dad said. The winter wore on late, but even through the bitterest days we worked, cutting the fingers out of our gloves so we could hold the nails. Carson wandered around the jobsite picking up cutoffs and scrap, throwing them into the burn barrel, and Moses kept close to her. My mom even helped out, brushing snow off lumber, sweeping the plywood floors, holding boards while my dad ripped them. When the house was dried in we could work even if it was snowing. We put in some of the floors. We used cheaper oak, even though neither my dad nor I much cared for the roughness of its grain. We put heart pine in the kitchen, and even unstained I could tell it would mellow, like my dad said, to such a human color that we'd always have our own favorite boards.

The room he called his study, though, which was really a kind of living room and dining room with bookshelves, was the place we would sit on upturned five-gallon Sheetrock dope buckets and drink coffee and stare at the walls and windows and tell ourselves what kind of a house we were building. He'd finished that room before so many other things were done, before he started any of the other rooms, because, he said, he had to have a place to think. We even laid the trim in. He said he couldn't wait. With the trim up, we could see the truest beauty of the house, because that wood would always show. The mitered joints had to fit perfectly, the trim nailed without a single hammer track. This was when I learned just how alive wood was, how it could be eased into place, when sixteenths of an inch were too crude a measure, the breaking points, the resilience, the ways of splintering. On days things went wrong, like the day he found out they'd set the electrical boxes to a half inch everywhere, assuming all our walls were Sheetrock, we'd go in that study, to talk about what to do. It was the black walnut. The three bookshelf walls, the base, the crown, even the mullions and sills were custom milled of walnut, but still it wasn't enough. He'd have tables built of it, too, for the room, and he showed me where he'd put them. That was the thing about black walnut, it took whatever we were thinking or saying and absorbed it, so that every day the wood was more thoughtful, more complicated. Of course it was sad; the darkness of it was deep, and, like my dad said, any finish at all would only make it deeper. Even with the windows and a skylight, the weight of the room made me bow my head when I walked in. But the light didn't seem like it came from the windows, or the skylight: it came from the wood; from underneath all that darkness, even on cloudy days, a warm, dusty light continually washed the sanded wood.

He kept an unfinished block of the walnut in the middle of the study, four feet high and as big around as when it was cut from the tree. He was going to carve something out of it, he said, one day.

I worked late into the nights until I was too tired to eat dinner. I didn't go to church anymore. I wondered whether I'd been going all along out of more fear than I'd realized. At the Mount Zion Primitive Baptist Church I'd gone to when I was seven, when we lived in Idaho, a Sunday School teacher once spent a whole month talking about nothing but Hell. He gave us peanuts that were too salty, then wouldn't let us go get a drink. He held up a glass of ice water that looked so delicious. Eternity, he said. You will wish it was this easy.

The man from the bank came to the jobsite. I went to the truck while he and my dad walked through the house, my dad putting his hand to the paneling, pointing out the beams, the piles of lumber, then they stopped for a long time in the kitchen, the empty kitchen. My dad hadn't ordered the cabinets; I knew about that. The company had changed the price from what they'd told him, just like the plumbers had done with the bathroom fixtures. My dad had said he might put shelving in the kitchen, just until we got through the main construction. We'd done so much on the house, and done it so carefully, but there were rooms—like the kitchen, the bathrooms, the garage, the closets, the laundry area—that still just had studs on the walls. Some of the floors were still plywood, and we still didn't have any heat. And the septic field should have been done, too, but my dad knew where it was going, and they could put it in without having to get behind the house.

They talked a while on the stoop, and I held my hands to the burn barrel. There had been times when the sawing and hammering sounds kept going, even after we stopped working. That happened now. And with the man from the bank there, I knew, trying to edge in some of his pale questions, holding out our draw like a glass of ice water, I heard even more—my dad telling me about the money, his words flying like mad bees, the men at the bank clicking their thin tongues, my mom and Carson calling me.

I went into the truck, where I could shake my head, and the noise stopped. I smelled the ashes of the last cigarette my dad had finished on the way to the house, a very faint trace of aftershave, and a strong flavor of coffee. Two brown glass coffee cups lay on the floorboard, along with dozens of scraps of paper. Some, the notes written in pencil in my dad's uneven handwriting, had been tightly crumpled. Different colored papers, with company names printed across the top, cataloged long lists of lumber and strange materials that I barely recognized: hardware cloth, cut nails, j-hangers. Code words; shorthand symbols written in the hurried slant of the lumber salesmen. Past due notices.

The flames in the burn barrel flickered, then locked. Paralysis took my muscles, the monotonous jet drone began, my neck stiffened. A white light moved away, like the pieces of a puzzle coming apart. The air tasted green, like after rain. A voice, soft and canyon-deep, vibrated in the bones of my head.

I saw my dad's mother, but it was a face I had never seen. At first, I could only make out fine wrinkles. An eyebrow, heavy. Fiery hair. Colors mottled and moved. Then I felt the hungry breath. Then the eyes; my heart beat wildly: the poverty sank in her firebrick eyes. Then a hand lay on my back, so heavy that it bent my bones.

Through the streaked windshield of the truck, the labyrinth frame of the unfinished house stood starkly against the woods. The fire in the burn barrel had grown even higher. I thought I saw a lick of flame touch one of the garage wall studs. In an instant, a translucent orange fire raged up the timbers, under the floor and around the joists. Ashes flew in gray clouds that kept disappearing, as though the house were exhaling deep breaths. Someone moved inside; the shadows of my dad and mom ran frantically through the house, trying to douse the flames but the water they were pouring ignited instead.

When I opened my eyes, my dad stood beside the truck, pouring a cup of coffee. The fire was gone, the smoke cleared. Now nothing moved against the naked whiteness of the house's bare timbers. Where only moments ago clean flames had washed it with dozens of fire colors, now it stood as it had before, except it seemed bleached, hardened: dead. The thought of the house set on fire lingered, ticklishly, in my lower abdomen. I did not know why I would even dream of such a thing. My dad did not seem to notice that I was still in the truck; he took a long drink from the steaming cup and watched the house like it was a television.

He said the men from the bank would steal it if we weren't careful. I wondered how that could happen, that they could take a whole house but never have to learn how to hold a saw. Even Mr. Duncan had been able to do that.

An Accident

"MOVE HER! YOU'VE GOT TO LET HER KNOW that you're not afraid. That's it...easy now, just keep turning her the way you want to go." I guided Delilah clumsily around the back yard, holding the reigns awkwardly high. My dad walked beside me, holding the harness. Sweat shimmered on the horse's flat shoulders. Near the corner of the back porch, Moses curled in the afternoon sun. Carson rubbed her swollen belly. Delilah shivered, and I started.

My dad led us to the driveway. "Easy now. Don't scare her." When he brought Delilah home, without warning, I was dumbstruck. It was the only prayer I could think of that had been answered. My dad had led her from the trailer, and when I got close enough to smell the wetness of her hair, I realized how tall she was. Carson ran up to her immediately, holding out her hand for the horse to smell. I stayed back. My dreams, of crossing deserts and riding at a gallop through underbrush, grew up, suddenly, replaced by a cold fear of the enormous, flinching animal. From the beginning, she had regarded me warily, reacting unpredictably to my movements. I rode only when I had to, when my dad got the notion that I might be short on grit. Otherwise I avoided her, except for dropping the buckets of water at her stall each morning.

"Hey cowboy! You new in town?" My mom slipped out the back door and waited for me to turn toward her. She swatted my leg as I rode past. "You look good up there. Are you having fun?"

I nodded. My dad let go of the harness. I nudged the reins lightly, trying to coax Delilah out to the field, but she trudged toward the house again. "No," I whispered. I pulled the reins harder, but not enough. As we swayed toward the house, Moses stretched in the sunlight while Carson poured her a saucer of milk in the grass at the edge of the porch. Delilah continued in a slow circle around the back yard, halting occasionally as though she were riderless, lowering her head for a mouthful of grass, then shaking her mane before she began walking again. I loosened the reins and decided to let her roam. I tried to breathe softly so as not to disturb her, and gradually I began to feel my legs relax, to enjoy the easy motion of her gait. My dad and mom stood by the truck, where they had unrolled the blueprints of the house; I could hear my dad explaining the kitchen, shaking his head.

"Hey," I waved to Carson.

"Why don't you take her somewhere?" Carson lifted Moses from the porch, draping her over her arm, and placed her beside the milk dish. "You're just going in circles. Why don't you ride her down to the spring and get the water for dinner?"

Delilah turned back from the house, facing the pasture. I leaned forward and whispered, "You want to go for a little ride?" I nudged her with my heels. She twisted, then broke into a slow trot. "Whoa," I called, trying to keep my voice low but hearing the stiffness in it. She slowed, rounding the corner to the back porch. Still sparked, she walked with a slight jump in her legs, and I tried to pull the reins. She twisted again. Carson shooed her, but still she headed toward the porch.

I tried to turn her again, but she continued, too close to the house, and I realized that I was about to knock my head against the overhang. I ducked quickly, pushing my hand into Delilah's back. She bucked sideways, even closer to the porch. Someone called my name through a fog. Then a cold shriek cut through, sinking into my stomach like a fist. Delilah jerked her head like she'd been bitten.

Moses was trapped beneath one of her hoofs. I fell in a crouch to the ground, not two feet from the cat, who dragged herself under the porch, meowing in broken breaths, her eyes stretched wide and frantic.

She was dead by the time Carson found her. Her coat was unmarked, but the body hung crookedly from Carson's hand and the teeth were wet with blood. As Carson and my mom went to the barn for a shovel, I held my hair in clumps, straining to keep my head still. The kittens, too, I thought; they might even still be alive inside her. They would die in her dark belly, and nothing I could ever do would make up for it.

I tried to cry, but all I could think of was the lilac tree at the gate to the pasture, where a while back my mom had chopped off the head of a black snake with the shovel. We would bury Moses there and when we moved and another family rented the house, the animals would be left behind, buried in someone else's yard. Later, when my mom and dad and Carson went back into the house, I stood in the pasture, a stone's throw from Delilah. I wanted to pray, so badly that I felt my heart go weak, but I could not think of anything to pray for.

No one blamed me. Even Carson, for days afterwards, brought me water at the table, waited for me after school, and walked with me to the property to find trees for tree houses. My mom took the buckets of water to the shed for Delilah in the mornings. Night after night, as I tried to sleep, I played over and over the scream of the cat, and I tried to pray. But I could not make words, and each night I fell asleep with a coldness in my chest that felt like a hand that had always covered my heart had been taken away.

I worked at the new house all the time now, sometimes with my dad, sometimes alone, losing myself in the rhythm of shoveling, of lugging cinder block, of keeping the floors perfectly clean. Sunday night I lay exhausted, squeezing my eyes shut, an icy sweat standing on my forehead. I had not yet taken off my clothes, and the sawdust in them tingled. I had worked furiously all weekend, but when my dad came to see what I'd done, it seemed like nothing, and I felt all our money dripping through my hands. The harder I tried, the more mistakes I made, and even though my dad never yelled, I could tell that every mistake mattered. I begged to feel the hand of God on my shoulder, just for a moment. When I woke up, suddenly, I was pinned to my bed. A hand had come to me as I slept. My skin from the center of my chest to my groin still tingled from the touch, heavy and light at the same time. God, I whispered. I followed the trail with my own hand, pushing where it pushed, drawing small circles, and then— my breath now came quickly—staying still. There was no sound, no light, nothing but the thick, salty air.

I sat up with a start, pulling the sheets down; I was naked.

I put my hand against the white of my skin. My hand was brown and rough like it belonged to someone older. I lay back down, exploring. My head rocked gently on the pillow, and it was almost like someone else was there with me, rocking with me, holding me.

I didn't know if what I was doing was wrong or right. Only a couple of nights before, Moses had crept in my bed and licked my wrists. Now I felt again her dry tongue, but this time under my skin. Everything was happening so much all at once, the noises and the naked exhaustion, and now the hardness, it all tingled and burned and sounded and moved, waiting for me to move my hand again between my thighs. I wanted more but it was all so bottled up. I wasn't old enough to make it let go, or to know when to stop.

The man from the bank had called again. My dad and I came home from working that evening, and my mom told us when she set our dinner plates on the table. "I'm too tired," my dad said, holding his head by the hair over his plate.

"Well, I'm sorry I brought it up," she said. That wouldn't be all she said, I knew from her voice.

When he raised his head, it looked like the muscles in his jaw were pulling his face apart. He laid his hand to the table quietly, but so hard that the legs creaked. "I'm just asking," he said. "Just not tonight. I'm tired."

She put a hand on my shoulder. "And what about him? You think you're tired, have you even looked at him? He's got circles under his eyes every morning when he wakes up. He's not even thirteen years old and you're working him like he's a full-grown man. It's too much. His teacher says he's spending more and more time nodding off, daydreaming. He doesn't hear half of what anyone says."

More Like Not Running Away

I could hardly hold my head still. The edges of her words caught, but they blurred, like her voice was coming through a long cardboard tunnel. She wasn't screaming. She kept her chin high.

"What in the goddamn hell is going on here?" He pushed his fork away and leaned forward. "I've been working all goddamn day, I come in to eat, in peace, and the next thing I know you're pounding the goddamn table. I asked you to leave me alone. Please."

But I knew that it was too late—too late for him to eat, because his muscles were already clenched, from his throat to his hands, and too late for her to stop talking, because she was scared to leave him so knotted up. "You answer the calls, then," she said.

"You can tell that little candy ass from the bank—" his voice rumbled in the wood of the table, in the plaster of the walls, and settled in the bones of my chest.

"Well, don't tell me. Tell him." She bit the words. "You read the letters." She grabbed an envelope from the window ledge, waving it. "Another one today. You've got to stick by the contract. They're not giving you any more money. It's not the kind of thing you can bully someone into doing. They want to see it done."

I wanted to run so badly, but I couldn't even move my hand from my lap. I tried to swallow. My mom arched at the table again. Heat ran from the corners of my dad's mouth.

"You don't get it," he said. "They've seen the house, and they know what it's worth. They'd love nothing more than to get their hands on it, to turn around and sell it for twice what they've got in it."

She laughed at the envelope. "Why don't you just read what they say? It's simple. Do you really think they want that house, to sell to who? Someone else to finish? Someone else who wants to throw money at copper flashing and black walnut paneling?"

The veins in her forehead rose. My dad had a white fist pushed to the edge of the table. His voice now shook in the floor. "Don't you attack me, I'm warning you. You know better. You know."

"Go ahead," she screamed now, "You want everyone to know, you want the blood in your eyes to show! Well, go ahead. Show them. Tell them."

He threw the table from under my arms. With one easy swing, the plates, glasses, forks, knives, the platter of cold meat, the bowl of mashed potatoes, all crashed into the wall and slid to the floor. The noise froze in my spine. The table lay against the wall. Splatters of food dotted the windows, the baseboards, the wallpaper.

Carson turned, and I could hear nothing but her soft footsteps on the stairs. My mom took a breath like a choke. I stood, and went to the door.

He walked to within inches of my mom. I braced, ready to rush back into the room to pull him off her. Then he lowered his head. Quietly, meanly, he said "You know this about me. You know what makes me do this, and you know it makes me sick. If you wanted a doctor with a Mercedes coupe and a brick ranch in a goddamn subdivision you could have had one. I've never laid a hand on you. If that's what you're waiting for, you know better."

Of course, I'd always known that's who he was, like I'd known even before he'd told me how a Skilsaw could rip a man's leg open. But always before, their voices cut at each other, back and forth. Not this time. This time, I only heard him dropping his hand. I only heard how hard it was not to touch her.

More Like Not Running Away

The next day Carson went to a friend's house. We were supposed to work on the house, but when I woke up it was after nine. Downstairs, the table was still on the floor, the dishes and food still where they'd been the night before. I went back upstairs to get dressed. Out of the corner of my window I saw my dad had backed a horse trailer to the pasture gate. I couldn't see him, though, so I put on some clothes and stepped out on to the roof. The sky was solid gray, and the air had the kind of winter to it where I knew it would get colder, not warmer, as the day came on. I could hear my dad's muddle of profanity from across the pasture. He was walking toward Delilah, but she kept shinnying away. I looked for my mom. Nothing else moved, though, except my dad and the horse.

He moved, Delilah moved. He slapped the reins against the rails. Suddenly, Delilah bolted, running far away from him, her legs flying almost magically over the ground, rocking her head and sending shivers up her mane. At the other end of the pasture she came to an easy halt, shivered all over, then started running again, but now not as much away as just in a free loop. But she did not go near my dad. He was walking to the truck, and when he got there, she stopped in the middle of the field like she was listening to something.

The truck started. The engine roared—he must have had the accelerator pushed to the floor. It died off for a moment, then it picked up again as the truck and horse trailer pulled through the gate into the pasture. Clods of dirt and grass flew from the back wheels of the truck, spitting up on the trailer. He was going faster and faster now, the back of the truck fishtailing, the trailer going opposite. The whole thing hit ruts and bottomed out then bounced back. Delilah stood until he came close to her, then she bolted again. He swung the truck and trailer to follow her, gunning the engine, going full speed. He came closer to her, then she swerved. He followed, but the truck and trailer took more space to turn. The trailer scraped a fence rail, opening a gouge in the side.

He didn't stop. He went again to Delilah before she cut away, but this time the truck thudded against a tree, the sound vibrating through the whole tree, the whole truck caught in a momentary shiver. My dad's head bounced off the side window.

He spun the truck in circles, over and over, not even close to Delilah. Thawed mud came up from his back wheels in small arcs. After a while, he drove out of the pasture, through the fence, splintering the rails. Delilah stood at the far corner of the field, her breath steaming, her neck shivering.

Then he got out and stood, sweating just like Delilah, opening and closing his hands. I think sometimes that if I'd gone out right then and thrown myself at him, taking him on barehanded, even if he'd had to throw me down, it might have saved all of us. There have been times when I secretly wished he'd actually killed Delilah that day, that it all could have ended right there.

"Don't move," I whispered. Carson slid one of her legs over, out of the shade into the sunshine. I held one of the Popsicle sticks over her broken stable as carefully as a scalpel, judging just the angle I'd need to lower it. She rose to her hands and knees, moving slowly, the way she moved toward animals.

"You forgot about the door," she said. "I had a door on this side."

"Why didn't you say something before?"

"I don't care," she said. "This is stupid."

"Why's Mom making you put this back together anyway?"

She rolled her eyes. "She saw me kick it."

"Why'd you do it?"

She turned toward the pasture. "It was mine. We don't need it anymore, anyway."

Just out of sight, down the dirt road, an engine roared. "He's home," she said. The blue pickup raced around the curve, braked suddenly, and then turned into the driveway. I grabbed Carson's hand and pulled her around to the side of the porch, away from the driveway.

"I've got to tell you something," I said. "It's not good."

She narrowed her eyes at me. "He's not slowing down."

The truck roared right up to the house. "I know," I said. His footsteps thudded across the kitchen floor. They started talking, muffled at first, but then I could hear.

"I'm telling you what they said," his voice came from a pit.

My mom talked now, high and sparkling through the window glass. "If you take this away from me now—"

Fists banged the countertops, cupboard doors slammed. The voices went still. Then she started talking again, cutting through the murmers. "We're not putting it off. I'll go talk to them."

"I've been back twice now. What do you want me to do? They won't reschedule the loan. It's a bunch of shit. Let the lawyers have it."

"What's wrong with the loan we had? What was wrong with it? Didn't you read ..."

I leaned toward Carson just as the crashing started. "You want to go somewhere?"

"Why doesn't he just go," she said bitterly. She covered one ear as the voices inside picked up again.

"He needs us," I said.

"That's stupid," Carson glared. "He needs us so he

doesn't have to clean up his own mess when he turns over the table."

"It's not that," I said. "It's not—"

"You know," she said. "That's your problem." She stuck her foot against the small stable. "You think we're supposed to hang on to him. We're supposed to believe in him just because he says so. You worship him."

Late that night I crept from my bedroom window and walked a long time, to the new house. I climbed to the roof of it. I walked it over and over but I didn't have a single word to say. I came down. In the front rooms, a sad moonlight fell to the corners. I thought of crying and praying, but I closed my eyes and let my head nod me back.

The house had a kind of beauty that was too much for a house. The ceilings, the plywood floors, the walnut still rough in places, the arches, the twelve-inch exposed rafters: and then it hit me, it could have been a church. I ran my hand along the empty walls. The nakedness of the kitchen and bathrooms. Wires hung from the ceilings where someone else would hang lights. No furnace, no doors, still nowhere to get a drink of water. Nothing to interrupt the long perfect incompleteness of every room.

But I saw more than that. Gashes in the paneling, door casings ripped out. The windows at the back of the house smashed, the exposed copper pipes twisted. Sledgehammer holes in almost every sheet of plywood on the floors, and the sledgehammer itself sunken into the walnut paneling. The beams and rafters were splintered, like they'd been whipped with a sword. Everywhere I saw it now: room after room, Sheetrock and trim and doors where an iron rod, a digging rod, had been swung. In a back bedroom I found the rod, bent and jammed through the wall, all the way from inside to outside. It was so cold I could hardly pull away my hand.

Just Listen

NO ONE SAID ANYTHING about what he'd done to the house. I didn't even know if my mom had seen it. For two days I listened to every sound from the road—I didn't know if the bank was going to come to our house to take away our stuff, or if the police might come and arrest my dad, or if he'd just disappear, like he'd done in the Army. Then the second night, at dinner, he just told us that he figured we'd like the next house—it was in Florida, it had a pool. When he said it, it was like something at the table was broken and no one was sure yet if it mattered. "The live oaks," he said without looking up, "go right along the driveway. It's nice. It's got three bathrooms. Not but five years old. Guess that means the plumbing's still working, anyway."

My mom went into the kitchen without answering him. He looked after her, his lips still parted. Carson kept eating, moving her fork exactly the same way except now she was getting hardly any food on it.

"Great," Carson said.

My dad strained to ignore her. "I guess we'll be going to a new school," I said, hoping to keep Carson from saying anything else. She had one hand on her lap and the other on the table not more than three inches from his. Even though it was scratched up and the skin of her knuckles was rough, she still had a kid's hands, still a little fat.

He had put his fork down.

"That's great too," Carson said. "We'll creep into some place like stupid people who got lost on the road or something. All because of that stupid house, because it had to be perfect. Because," she looked directly at him, "you lost our money."

Without moving his eyes he raised his hand and brought it down with a soft smack on the back of hers.

She didn't flinch. "Because you wasted it."

Again he slapped her hand, this time hard enough that it showed in her eyes.

"I hate you," she said and he slapped it again. She kept talking, leaving her hand out for him, and he kept hitting her, harder and harder until she couldn't keep her face still any longer. Finally she stood up. "So now you can throw the table, or whatever you want," she said. "And what about Delilah? Yeah, I know. It's all just great."

His face had no color. She was still within reach. I recognized the blood in the air. I was afraid that if I moved in any way, whatever held them apart would break. When Carson finally turned to leave, his hands stayed right where they were.

"That," he said, "is the last I want to hear about the house. I've tried. I'm who I am."

He went to the door. My mom stood in the doorway, her

face dry, her eyes not at all red. "Don't ever put your hand on her again," she said. "I mean it. What you've done to this family—"

But he was gone, he'd walked past her without touching her.

He didn't say another word until the day we left. His silence was hard, and I could hear it the few times we were alone, as though the long explosion of what he wanted to say forced him to clench even his breath. The house got so quiet it was like we'd already quit living there. My mom always had a cup of coffee in her hand but she didn't ask me to stay up with her. Hours after I had gone to bed and had read or dreamed all I could, I'd slip down the old stairs and see the light on in the kitchen and smell the coffee and hear her light a cigarette. Once or twice she talked to someone on the phone, but so softly that I couldn't hear her. Someone came and drew Delilah into a trailer one day, and after that Carson didn't say anything either.

I kept going to school that week. They didn't know we were leaving and I didn't say anything. It took a while every morning for the noise of the place—the kids' high voices and the books and the doors slamming—to give way to the smaller sounds—the pencils scratching the paper, the teachers' soft shoes gliding back and forth on the terrazzo floors—but more and more I just let my head rock, nice and easy. Then home and school sounded the same. The noises came to me through a dozen cinder-block walls. Even when a teacher pulled me aside one day I let my head rock, letting her face blur in my eyes, while she asked if I'd seen the school nurse or a doctor. It's okay, I told her, it's okay, okay. And it was. I still turned in homework but I didn't look at any of the grades. I took quizzes and read and heard enough of what the teachers said, I held it together. I went outside at recess, and

let the sun on my face, and rocked, the silent music filling me
up. Every once in a while someone would nudge me, or try to
talk in my face, and I couldn't help the shiver, but they always
went away. Finally I was brought to one of the guidance
counselors and she said she'd make an appointment for me to
meet with someone, but I knew we'd leave Michigan before
that would happen.

A week after my dad tore up the house, a young sheriff's
deputy came to talk to him. For the first few minutes, I thought
he'd arrest him—I was hoping he would, until I caught myself.
Then I realized the deputy was just going to ask questions like
he already knew the answers. After a little while my dad's
voice went dead and the deputy took a sharp breath, and then
he backed toward the steps. He asked only two more questions
and didn't raise his eyes. I thought maybe he could tell my dad
was lying. But then he was moving like he was scared, even
though my dad hadn't moved at all. It was my dad's face. His
eyes weren't flashing like they usually did when he was angry;
his stare now was coiled, and he breathed through his nose.
This is what it looks like, I knew as instinctively as I knew my
own breath, *this is the face you see when the animal has you in his
teeth.* When the deputy left, my dad turned to me, like he could
finally say what he'd been bottling up. He opened his mouth.
He was breathing hard, almost desperately. You don't need to
tell me, I thought: I saw it.

I can't imagine how my mom had talked with my dad without
my hearing it. The morning after the deputy had been there,
she told me and Carson that the plans had changed now. "We're
not going to Florida," she said, "not right away. Your dad is,
he's going to start the job. But we're going to drive to Seattle,
to stay with Frankie for a little while. Till things settle down."

"Does he know?" I asked.

She nodded. "We'll have fun," she said. "We'll stop some places along the way. Maybe we'll even camp out—you know, just really take things easy. And," she folded her hands, "your dad, I think he needs some time, to think."

I could hardly hold myself still, thinking of camping out with my mom, almost like a real vacation, of being free from the house, from school, and of actually spending a while in a city, doing the things Frankie liked to do, going places just for fun.

Carson had been quiet for so many days by now that I'd forgotten how small her voice could be. "Mom," she said, "that sounds so good. I wish—I wish," she struggled for a word, "I've been scared a lot."

"Honey, he—" But my mom couldn't finish, I knew.

"And I love Aunt Frankie. But do you think I could stay with Grandma and Grandpa?" She said it quickly, and waited.

"In Indianapolis? I don't understand," my mom said. "Is there something wrong, something wrong with staying with us?"

Carson shook her head. "It's just I've been thinking about it for a long time, all week, about how I could go there. And they have a room I could have to myself, and Blink."

Blink was their dog, a St. Bernard that would sleep right in Carson's bed when we'd visit.

"The dog," my mom said slowly. "Oh, I see." Carson's face was so full of wanting that it hurt to see it. My mom went over and put her arms all the way around Carson's head. "Oh, baby," she said, "I know exactly what you mean. I think we can work it out. I think Blink might be just the right thing. Let me talk, to them, and to him."

They both cried, just a little, while they hugged. They were smiling, too, and I almost went over to where they were. "We'll get you there somehow," my mom said.

Later that morning my mom took me to a restaurant for coffee. We talked about camping, about Seattle, and mom said she thought Carson had a good head on her shoulders.

"Mom," I said finally, "about what Dad did, to the house. Is he in trouble? Are they going to arrest him or something?"

"Honey," she said, "right now things are pretty mixed up. What happened with the house, that's not just a money problem, it's not just that. Your dad," her voice started drifting, "he's going to have to come to terms with a lot of things."

"Like what happened in the Army, right?" I pleaded.

"Yes."

"When, when he was in the Army, did he have to go to jail ever?" The question seemed to take all the air from around us.

She put her hand to my chin. "What I'm telling you now is what he did to the house, the bank's going to want us to pay for that, and he can't just raise his voice or go in there like he's going to start shooting and think they're going to let it go. But it's not just money. He's—" she tried to draw what she wanted to say with her hands but they just made empty motions.

She let her hands down. "He did go to jail, for a while. But that's not what I'm talking about. He's saying things now that worry me. God, I'm not trying to scare you, baby," and she moved to my side of the table and put her arm around me. I was still trying to catch her words, to make sure that she had really said that he'd been in jail.

"Please don't be scared. But he's saying things about what happened before, and about the bank, and I think it's all getting mixed up in his head." She winced. "He's got to be careful."

"Mom," I said, "I'm going with him." The words came out

like they had when I preached, like they weren't even my words.

She let go of me. "No. No you don't say that. Carson, that's fine. I understand that. But not you. There's no way."

But of course, what could she say? We didn't even argue, she just kept saying no until she ran out of it.

She left that night, her suitcase pulling down her shoulder, and I couldn't take my eyes from the empty doorway. I waited until the wanting, to run after her, to pull her back from the driveway, faded with her down the street. When I couldn't hear her car anymore, I went upstairs, to my bedroom. She left Carson with us, with me and my dad, since we were going through Indianapolis anyway, and I felt a little better that she trusted me enough to do that. I went to bed early that night, our last night in the house, but never did sleep. I just heard her voice, over and over, through the walls.

You grew up so quickly, she'd said to me the day I came in from helping my dad pack away the tools from the site of the house after we lost it. Your eyes get wider every day here, you've seen so much. Places in this country I never imagined existed when I was a little girl, earthquakes and oil well fires, remember where the jet crashed right down the road from our house in Oregon? We heard it, a thud through the ground that I just knew wasn't natural. Over a hundred people were killed, and every day we'd drive by and for months we could still see shoes and scraps of clothes in the trees, purse straps and belt buckles, the black grass and branches, and the ground all ripped apart. Sightseers came and took every last thing they could find. But you were only what? two years old? You don't remember now but you cried at the smell of it, the burned-up everything. You don't remember but you were there, there was no way to keep from passing it—right on the road where we lived! Now I look at you and sometimes I remember like it was a second ago that you were my whole life, a baby that took my breath away. Your daddy just out of the Army and we'd drive days and days across the country with you and you never cried once, you stared out that window like those trees and mountains and cornfields were little parts of you that you wanted to reach out and grab back. He absorbs everything, your daddy said, he won't stop watching from the time he gets up till he goes to bed. I don't know to this day what you saw out there. I would hold you in my arms for hours while your daddy drove that old Plymouth with no idea where we were going from one day to the next. You've just seen and seen, some things I was glad for you to see—the churches in every town we ever stayed in, I do think those people were good, they listened and let you be, and that chapel in Santa Fe—were you too young then? you know, with the little round staircase that they said was a miracle—when was it we saw that? I'll ask your daddy, I know we did. And things I should have kept from you, things not fit for a child's eyes and especially not for you, you just could never seem to close your eyes. How you just cave in when you see your dad screaming out of here in that truck, kicking gravel right up to the windows, I know, it scares me too and to think that you've had to sit in that truck, just a baby, on his wild rides.

Early that morning, before the sun even came up, I opened the window that opened to the roof but I didn't go outside, I didn't preach, I didn't hear anything.

part **Two**

I have heard all things in my life. I've heard God, and the silence God leaves behind.

They've told me that space is so empty that it can't carry sound, but that's not true. I know, there was a time when new rocks split and fused, when the planets and suns all flew free of one another, when every note rang across the universe in constant harmony with every other note. When God took his first breath, he took in all the noise of creation, so sometimes we think the space between us and the stars is empty, but no—if you listen, it still rings.

Why Things Are
the Way They Are

THE THREE OF US GOT INTO THE TRUCK. On the way down to Indianapolis my dad took tight, anxious breaths, like he could not get enough air to say what he wanted to say. Carson didn't talk about Delilah. Losing Delilah was a part of moving, losing things was always a part of moving, selling things, giving things away. My dad drove like ice, down the flat Michigan and Indiana roads without blinking, keeping the engine at a steady airplane whine, holding the steering wheel with both hands except to smoke. No one touched the radio.

When we dropped Carson off at the brown wooden house in Indianapolis, she trudged up the front steps and disappeared. Our grandparents were quiet people. They didn't drink or smoke or read books or raise their voices. The house looked like it did in the pictures of my mom when she was a girl. My dad and I stayed long enough to bring Carson's two suitcases to the back porch, then we left. For the next several hours, until we stopped for dinner at the Indiana-Kentucky border, I could only think of Carson's small, thin back going up those steps. Her legs were still little girl's legs with droopy socks and broken skin, tough legs with bigger muscles than mine, but with something glass about the bones. "She's eleven, Everest," my mom said only a few weeks ago. "She does what eleven-year-olds do; try to remember that and let her grow up."

Carson had gone up the stairs with a quietness that I did not know in her. Even though we'd lived so long in the same houses, I didn't know what made her move or talk or what made her want to hold on to animals the way she did, animals that never seemed to last any longer than schools or friends or houses. Her face was as familiar to me as my own, but now when I tried to hold the picture of it in my mind, it slid away.

Without Carson in the truck, I thought my dad might say what he always said when we moved, that *Things would be different this time,* that we would do things in the new place that we didn't do before, go on hikes and take vacations. I had quit believing that, but now, even though I knew it would be a lie, I wanted to hear it. My mom and Carson both left like it didn't matter, like they were going into another room, but for the first time, I was realizing that they might not come back. I thought of this for a few hours in the quiet of the truck, letting myself miss them, and then the sadness just went away.

Living without them might be something we could do. There would be nothing to fight about anymore. There would be hours and hours after school to just read, and me and my dad would go out every night for dinner and my dad would start telling me the things he never had time to tell me before, about the time in the Army, or how to fire people. We might even give up the house and live in an upstairs apartment with a balcony. The more I thought about it the more I saw we could make it work, so much that I could hardly keep from saying it all out loud. I thought about it from every angle, how we could move and move and I would never complain.

But I said nothing. We drove all night through the middle states, Kentucky, Tennessee. They went by dimly, not the trees or grass or shapes of buildings but only a humming of the road, rising and falling. I slept sometimes, laying my head down on the seat of the truck near my dad's lap until my breath was full of oily cigarette and vinyl and the tired smell of the hours. With my eyes closed, I could feel through the seat the movements my dad was making—cracking the window to let out the smoke, pushing the accelerator or touching the brake, tipping the steering wheel, reaching for cigarettes. We took long breaks at rest stops where my dad didn't sleep but drank coffee from his Thermos and smoked while I slept or looked out the window. As we crossed into Georgia, the air got heavy with a moistness that I could feel when I rolled down the window.

Midmorning in south Georgia, the light came over the tops of the pine trees. The road opened. The night in the truck wore off in the warmth. Clumps of trees with night between them gave way to shacks and fences, then long lines of trees that were too tall to pick from.

"Why are those trees in lines?" I hadn't even thought before I'd spoken.

"These?" He nodded toward the rows of trees, planted widely apart, diagonal to the road.

"Yeah, they run off in straight lines." Occasional houses, surrounded by narrow fields, broke the pattern.

"Pecan groves." He was nodding; his voice was easy.

"Those houses are tiny. Do people live in them?

"They do. All the time."

More Like Not Running Away

The houses stood on stilts, open underneath. They didn't sit squarely with either the road or the trim rows of pecan trees on either side of them, as though they'd been dropped to the ground. Some backed directly to a row of pecan trees, scrunched from the open spaces to a corner of the grove.

"Because," he explained, "they don't own the houses. Sharecroppers, migrants mostly. They stay there and work the groves. So if the owner loses a row of trees to a road or wants to expand, he'll put in a new row wherever he can—right around a house if he has to. Or tear the house down."

"Why don't people just move somewhere else?" Some of the houses were mobile homes, with wheels still under them.

"They could, but these people don't think there's anywhere to go. People who live like that," he waved his hand, "live like that. And they never think about getting the hell out." Dirt roads led up to them and past them, I guessed on to other houses even more remote, maybe even poorer. Roofs were caved in. Everything about a house would slope, even porch posts and windows. Entire houses were whopperjawed almost to the point of falling over to one side, like they'd been wrenched by a gigantic hand. Walls buckled, leaving gaps in the siding large enough that a person could reach right inside. There were no yards, just spaces littered with toys and old lawnmowers, burn barrels, tires, piles of things rusting, half sheds, and cars parked up to the front doors.

And between the houses, we passed mile after mile of trees in perfect rows with belts of soft grass underneath. My dad was talking now, about the ways of being poor, of clean poor and dirt poor, of black and white poor, he reminded me of the different ways of being poor in the cities, old people eating canned dog food and children who never ate a hot meal. He talked about the ways he had been poor, how it was like heat in that it stuck to the skin and wouldn't come off, and that being poor was dreaming day and night, if you were smart enough to dream. People who saw you would always move their heads a little—sometimes to turn away, sometimes to look down.

We'd lived in old houses, and I knew there had been times when my mom couldn't pay our bills, but we'd never been poor. I had new boots and jeans from JCPenney's every year, and I'd seen my mom put five dollars in the Salvation Army bucket at Christmas, more than once. My dad had protected us from the poverty he had said he couldn't ever seem to run away from. And that morning, leaving the sharecropper shacks behind us, I think he felt like he could talk again because he knew he'd done it, he'd kept us out of trailer parks and mill towns. He was talking again at last. And I was there.

Early in the afternoon we drove through the half dozen stores that made up Sopchoppy in the Florida Panhandle. We checked into a ten-room motel backed up to the woods. By then the sun was blurring off the truck hood and through the windshield. We lay on the thin beds with our clothes still on, and I looked out the window at the hairy webs of Spanish moss hanging hot on the trees. We had carried in only two suitcases and just during the short walk from the truck to the motel room the sweat grew sticky on my skin. The air didn't move. The trees grew closer together here than anywhere I'd ever seen, some of them no higher than a single house, thick from the soggy ground, the limbs covered with vines. Nothing seemed to grow in its own place, it just took up what empty space it could find. Some of the trees grew so crooked, with their branches bent into the crowded underbrush, that they looked like they wanted to fall over and die. They were live oaks, my dad said. The crookedness was part of their beauty.

More Like Not Running Away

We turned on the air conditioning unit under the window when we checked into the room, but even after the bedsheets cooled off they were sticky and damp.

"How old are you?" He lay on top of the bedsheet and pulled a long time on his cigarette.

"I just turned thirteen a couple of weeks ago."

"I've got to tell you something."

I picked up a broken-off air conditioner knob from the windowsill. I held it just over my head, turning it back and forth in the air.

"What happened up there, in Michigan, I can't live that way anymore. I've spent the last fifteen years of my life running, scared to death I was going to do it again. I tried to build a place where I could forget, a place to live that was so beautiful I could forget that I was ever poor, that I'd ever done the things I'd done. But it collapsed on me, just like everything else."

"Do what again?" I could barely speak. "You're scared to death you're going to do what again?"

He breathed easy. "I want you to know. I want you to know why things are the way they are."

There was a diesel engine running outside the motel window, it ran and ran until it was all I could hear. Like rain, his story came on, and I remembered some parts I had heard before but now they drenched me. I listened, but my dad's voice might as well have been coming from the television because I was as alone as I'd ever been in my life.

"I'd run as far away from Laurinburg, North Carolina, as I knew how. Not being able to read, every street sign, every menu, stopped me dead in my tracks. You can't imagine, sitting in a laundry room wondering how the goddamn machine works.

"The Army sent me to sniper school. They gave us manuals on a rifle and wanted us to tear them apart and put them back together. That wasn't any problem. Not half the guys in the room even looked at the manuals, but the guy teaching it, named Ashe, Sergeant Ashe, he wouldn't have it. Said we had to do it again, by the book. And he's walking around behind us, seeing are we reading it? And I'll be goddamned if he doesn't come up behind me, studying me like I was a disease.

"'Go on,' this bastard says, 'listen up, ya'll! Private Revel here's going to read this part here for us now.' And he waits."

I'd been spinning the air conditioning knob back and forth over my head this whole time, for no reason.

"Are you listening?" he asked.

I said I was. I let the knob fall to my chest, but I didn't move it away. I hadn't thought about it directly, but I knew vaguely that fiddling with it like I was would irritate him.

"And that's what started it." He turned away from me now. "I should have knocked his teeth out right there. Maybe then, the rest wouldn't have happened, like it did. Maybe I should have gotten in his face. Who the hell knows. But I guess at that point I was thinking, I hadn't put up with all that Army shit for a year already just to get myself locked up with a bunch of flunked out losers."

"Have you ever knocked out a person's teeth?"

He turned, frowning. "What the hell are you talking about?"

I turned the knob back and forth on my chest.

"I read you can put teeth back, when they get knocked out," I said. "You can just stick them back. Where they came from."

He acted like he didn't hear me. After a while he breathed hard through his teeth. "I didn't live on the base. It was one thing, I had to have someplace decent I could go to. I got this apartment in the part of town where some of the junior officers lived. Nothing fancy—pretty run-down, I guess, looking back on it—but quiet. And respectable. So I'm coming home, and there that son of a bitch is. Right outside my door.

"'You know,' this son of a bitch says, 'if you can't read, kid, they got programs for it. They even teach the halfway retards to do it.'"

My dad stuck his cigarette out on the table. "I'm going to tell you something," he said to me. "I'm going to tell you something." Then he didn't say anything for what seemed like a long time. But I knew. I could just picture what kind of man would be so stupid as to say that to my dad, some sorryfaced guy with slow eyes and bits of whiskers he forgot to shave.

"When I hit that kid Edgar," I said, "I did like what you said to do. You know, I—"

"You're listening," he said, like I hadn't been. "'Listen,' I told him. I said, 'Hey man, you don't want this. Go on and leave me be.' I tried to tell the son of a bitch, I tried to tell him but he wouldn't hear me, he keeps talking right on into the building, and when he starts up the steps, still talking his shit, I couldn't hardly keep my hands still. I get right outside my door, telling myself just hold on, just get inside.

"Then he says, right at my ear, 'Ain't it just like you illiterate morons, can't see even when somebody's trying to steer you right. Well, go on. I seen plenty of losers before, I'll see plenty more, too.' And he's pointing at me while he's talking. I told him one last time, to back off, and he spits, right on the rug at my feet."

I wanted to listen to my dad so bad. Through all the waiting and wondering of the last few months I'd figured out most of what he was going to say, but I didn't know the details, and I wanted to know all of them. The problem was, right then, maybe because of the drive, or the lousy room, I didn't want to hear him saying it. His words were all coming out way too slow, the way he'd talked about the house so much, like I was supposed to be memorizing whatever he said.

But I couldn't say anything to him. I started trying to fit the knob back on the air conditioner.

He didn't notice. He wasn't even looking at me, he was talking to the far parts of the room, glancing in the mirror every now and then. "I'm standing ten inches taller than him. By the time the bastard looked up, he knew. He could see he'd gone too far. He starts making little motions in the air with that finger, saying *Man, don't do it.* He goes to step back, but there's the stairs behind him. I reach out nice and easy and take his finger just like this," he turned his hand like he was pushing a lever, "and bend the finger back. All the way. You could hear it pop. He goes down to his knees, and I put my leg against his face, shove him into the wall.

"That's when he bites me. My leg. I couldn't even feel it. But I saw the blood running down his mouth, I knew what it was. I pull back, kick him right under the ribs. He goes down the stairs, to the landing. He's in a pile. You'd of thought I'd quit then. No. I—I—"

My dad barely had the air to make words anymore. His eyes were closed. "I go after him. There's his hand out on the floor, his finger already huge from getting broke. I step on it, and then I start kicking him. In the throat, jacking his head back. I couldn't quit. I couldn't. To this day I don't know what got a hold of me. Down the stairs. Into a corner. Like I was stomping in the mud.

"I seen all the colors in the cracks on the wainscoting. A hell of a thing to be looking at when you're kicking a man to death though, ain't it? But things were that slow. And I'll tell you another thing. I was begging God the whole time to make me quit. I'd been doing everything right. Here I'd left Laurinburg, made a new start. And all it took was about thirty seconds to ruin my entire life."

I could not get the knob on. It didn't make any sense; it was so simple, just a hole in the knob with one flat side to it, and the stem matched it, round except one flat side. I'd turned it up, over, and pushed and kept pushing, harder. It slipped, and dropped to the floor. When I leaned over to pick it up, my dad stood up—I could hear him do it—and walked to where my hand was and put his heel on the knob and cracked it neatly into pieces. It hardly made a noise, and he didn't say another word, he just went back to his seat.

He tapped his forehead. "You see now." I thought he might say it hard but he didn't, he said it like nothing had happened, in the voice he saved to tell me good things, the voice he'd used that day he let me steer his truck. "You see what I mean, why I'm telling you. I got to fight that every day, knowing what I'm capable of. Looking at what I did to that man, I knew right then, they were all right about me, everyone who said I was no good, I mean—here I'd killed a man in cold blood—what worse could I do?

"You know, my mother would pray all the time, squeeze the blood right out of her hands, right up to the day she died. That's what I thought standing over that man. Here I'd worked all those years, done the best I could in the Army, and in less than five minutes, you know, it's all over. Wouldn't you think, I mean, if there ever was a time that God would give a shit about a man, he'd of been there?"

I didn't know why he was telling me about God now. And the way he was asking, it was like he really thought I would know what to say. I was remembering the fights with my mom, and the way the pale guy at the bank looked at him, and how other people had looked at him, and it all made sense.

"Go out to the truck and get me another pack of cigarettes, will you?" He lay back on the bed. The daylight outside stung my eyes. There didn't seem to be enough blood going to my head at first when I stood up, but now, in the truck, a hot redness flushed across my face.

I thought about just walking away, for good. I wondered if he came after me, if he'd be mad. But I'd never seen a place so tangled up with underbrush, with such hot empty roads, where someone could get so lost.

I pulled a pack of cigarettes from the glove box and thumped them against my palm. The dark smell of the Pall Malls was something about my dad I loved, like the power saws, and the stories about North Carolina. I turned the fresh pack in my hands, then gently pulled off the band around the top. My dad said that opening a new pack of smokes was easy and hard. It was easy because even when you were closer to forty years old, you still got to open a package of something just for yourself two or three times a day. It was hard because if you opened a pack in a hurry and tore off too much cellophane or forgot to tamp them down before you pulled off the foil, you had to live with the messed up pack. For a long time, he didn't like me or Carson to open them for him, because we didn't take the time to do it right. I held the little open square to my nose. I'd played with them often enough, tasting the white paper and nibbling bits of tobacco. I pulled one from the pack and stuck it in my fingers. I touched it to my lips. When the time came, I'd have my own packs to tamp on my palm, to light up when I started to say something. I'd drive the truck while my dad watched out the window talking and not talking, with the same sawdust under our boots, the same black coffee in our hands.

Back inside the room, I handed the cigarette to my dad and studied the match he lit it with.

"Does that ever hurt?"

He raised his eyebrows. "It gets easier."

I picked up the pack from the dresser again and started to flick one out. My dad kept his eye on me. "Go ahead." His eyes were still on me, through me. I picked up the book of matches from the dresser like I wasn't thinking about it and lit the cigarette. The smoke rolled in my mouth and I blew it out too hard. Then I just let it drift around my face a while and didn't think about it.

"Did you go to prison?" I asked him.

He nodded. "After I turned myself in, till they court-martialed me. That's who you're named after, you know, Jack Levi, the man who spoke up for me. He was running a program in the prison, trying to put together a group of us for details they couldn't use regular soldiers for. He's the one who really taught me how to read. He'd come by the cell and recite poetry, make me learn it. There's one I remember—

On the heights of great endeavor,
Where attainment looms forever,
Towering upward, ceasing never,
Climb the faithful centuries.
Joy and anguish in their faces,
On they strive, the living races,
And the dead, who no one sees.

"So anyway. He testified for me in court. I got put on his detail after the trial. That went on for the better part of two years, right after you were born."

For a while we didn't look at each other. It scared me that

he'd killed someone, and that he could tell me about it the way he did, the same way he talked about starting his own business, or making lots of money. I wished that instead of the cinder-block walls and aluminum windows and threadbare bedspreads, instead of the air outside being still and wet, that we could have been somewhere surrounded by wood and books, that we could have been in that walnut study we'd built. But the room by now was sour with the piles of smoked cigarettes.

"Your mom knows all about it," he said. "I told her, before we got married, exactly what I was. I told her I'd make sure my family never lived like lowlifes, that I'd never lay a hand on her. Or anyone else. And I've stuck to it.

"I hate people," he turned his palms up, "I can't stand small talk, and the shit people think is funny. Subcontractors too drunk to show up, superintendents with their asses on their shoulders—I get to where I can't listen to another goddamn word somebody's saying and that's it. I know when it's coming, and the only thing I can do is get out. I've never raised my hand to another human being since that day, and if I have to pick up and move from one end of the country to the other every day of my life, I'll do it. And I'll make a living."

I had smoked two cigarettes by now and my head craved air. The diesel engine outside the window kept humming, until it was all I could hear.

After a while he was asleep. I lay awake, and even though I got up twice to wash my hands they wouldn't quit smelling like the cigarettes. I finally took a cigarette from the pack that was in his shirt, over a chair, and went outside to smoke it, but I forgot a lighter. When I turned to go back in, the door had locked behind me. There was nothing I could do but sit on the curb outside the room. At least it wasn't cold out. If I started feeling sorry for myself I'd think about Delilah, Carson's horse. I never really wanted to ride her, mainly because horses scared me, but the buckets of water were too heavy for Carson, so I was the one who carried them out to the stall every morning. And every morning I'd look at her, right at her big horse eyes, and think that I ought to pet her, because all the time I was in a bed in our house, with covers and all that, and Delilah just had some hay and blanket that hardly covered her. On the really cold days I almost couldn't even look at her. But I always thought that it was Carson's business, being nice to the horse. I always thought I just had to do the water, and that it wasn't really fair.

That night I spent outside the motel room with a cigarette I couldn't light and the diesel engine running all night, what I wanted more than anything was to see Delilah just one more time, just to do what I should have done before, to put my hand to her face, to pet her, even if she shivered me away.

Easy, Cheetah

OF ALL THE PLACES WE'D LIVED, I knew right away that Sopchoppy would be the worst. It was already too close, too gritty in my clothes and scraping at my skin. My dad said the soil reminded him of the sandhills around Laurinburg, how it was loose and how the pine trees looked like they were sick. We drove down miles of sandy roads that ran point to point without turns, and crossed in the middle of nowhere, then dead-ended in the middle of nowhere. The roads drifted into this solid underbrush. None of the houses were next to each other, even the convenience stores and white cinder-block churches stood off by themselves. But it wasn't just how far apart things were; the brush went into the road and crawled right into people's yards, tangling up their old cars and swingsets. I looked for deer cuts, any breaks, but the only time it quit was when it came to the ditches of black water. I started thinking about ways through the underbrush, even if I had to cut through like an explorer with a machete. But we just kept driving, making the same turns, down more of the same roads.

At last we turned off one of the sand roads on to a long driveway. The house stood giant and yellow on an unmowed yard almost as big as a field. When I stepped out of the car, a swarm of blackstriped mosquitoes nipped at my neck, wrists, and knees.

"Needs some work." He flicked the rest of his cigarette into the tall grass. "Before your mother gets here." He hadn't said much since we'd left the motel that afternoon, and I was surprised at the gentleness of his voice.

We walked around back. A sagging chain-link fence went around the pool. The water was dirty and had stained the liner. The back yard was as big as the front yard, and some stray bushes came up in the middle of the grass. I reached my hand to the house; it was not stucco, like I'd thought, but a gritty yellow paint over cinder blocks.

No one had lived there for a while, I could tell. Inside it was stifling hot and smelled sour and wet. When he turned on the lights, some bugs disappeared into the corners, into a mess of cobwebs and brown dust. The kitchen was almost new, but some of the Formica had peeled from the edges of the counters. "Moving truck's coming this afternoon," he said. "The phone's on. You ought to call your mother. I've got to get to work."

When he left, I started a list of things I'd need to do—first cleaning, like my mom always did before the movers came, if I could find a rag or a broom. I needed to call someone to get the bugs, too. I'd have to cut the grass. First, though, I wanted to call my mom. At least by the time she got there, I figured I'd at least have the cobwebs cleaned up, and the grass mowed back so that things wouldn't look so wild.

"You don't sound so good," she said when I called. "Are

you sick?" The electric way she talked through the phone wires hummed warm against my ear.

"It's just quiet here right now." I leaned my head against the window jamb. "This is a good house, Mom," I said. "The kitchen's got all new cabinets, and a new sink, and refrigerator. And you know what? It's got a dishwasher. Really," and I touched the door of it like I could show her.

"Your Aunt Frankie's such a character." My mom laughed, a soft laugh that played over and over down in my ear. "She says hi, and you know, keep your eye on the ball. She's got pictures of baseball players everywhere—she even collects the cards—and you know she just has to go to all the games, to the Mariners. Have you heard of them? I had no idea she was such a baseball fanatic. So." Her words piled up fast and I closed my eyes to keep up with them.

"Anyway, guess what I'm thinking about doing?"

"What?"

"Well, they've got this little paper here called *Seattle Secrets*. They do all kinds of things, you know, places to go, what the local gossip is, stuff like that. Well. I have an idea, to write some things for that. I read this article yesterday about places to go inside when it's raining, and I thought, why not places to go outside when it's raining? I'm going to write it up and send it to them and see if they publish it. And I've got lots of other ideas too, I've just been thinking all day about it, like places to go to watch people fish, or places for indoor picnics, you know? I saw one just this morning, the lobby of a business building downtown with this beautiful fountain, you can sit right on the ledge and eat. I've got a list with at least a dozen ideas! I just have a feeling. I think this is something I can do. And I'd be able to get out, to meet people. It would be perfect for me."

I could see her wearing clothes like Frankie, wearing

lipstick and earrings, walking through the office buildings with a small green notebook, laughing with strangers, asking them questions, going to crowded baseball games with Frankie. The phone was hot now where it touched my ear. "When are you—" I asked, but the question melted.

"Levi," she said, her voice suddenly warm, "you have no idea how much I miss you. And Carson."

"I'm fine," I said. I leaned harder against the window jamb.

"I was thinking," she said, "you should go ahead and go to the school and get registered. Your shot records are in a shoebox—it's the one I always keep somewhere up high, they'll need to see those. It should only be, maybe three or four more weeks of school in the year. Then," she said even more softly, "well, I don't know, but you need to go ahead and get into school there."

"Mom," I said, "when are you—I mean, I was just wondering. If, you know, you're going to write all these articles there in Seattle, then when," but my words would not string together.

"Levi. I'm just not sure. I talked to Carson last night, and you know, for the first time in I don't know when, she sounded like she used to, she sounded happy. And right now, this is where I need to be. Doing what I'm doing. I don't know how long, but I'm just thinking that when you and Carson finish with school, you could come out here for a while, kind of like a little vacation. You know, I was realizing that we've never had a real vacation. Did you even realize that before? Maybe this is a good time for one. You could see the place we lived in when you were born—you know, you were born not all that far from Seattle. Anyway, Levi. Just think about it."

I knew now, with her voice sawing in and out, moving farther and farther away, that she would probably never see this house. Where I was sitting, the linoleum had been cut too short, so that it didn't reach the shoe mould. It wasn't any different from the motel we'd left that morning. "What should I tell Dad?"

"Well, I've been thinking about that, and here's what I guess I've been thinking. This could be a good time for him, too, to sort things out. He can call me, too, any time. He's got the number here, and at some point I guess he'll know better exactly where we're going. From here, I mean." She didn't say anything for a while then.

"Levi," she said, "I do worry about you down there. Alone."

Maybe, I thought then, she was worried about how to tell him she wasn't coming right away. "I'm fine," I said. "Don't worry about us."

"You can come here, if you want," she said. "I meant to say that right away, that if you want, we can fly you here, you can come stay here. You know I want you to."

"Mom," I said, tasting my breath against the phone receiver, "that's okay." She was waiting for me, I knew that, and I wasn't trying to make her wait, but I didn't have any words right then.

"I should go now," she said. "I miss you so much. I worry about you down there all alone, please, please be careful. Are you going to church?" She waited. "I know you can hear me. I love you."

"Mom," I said, but all the words were too huge.

"You get to know some of those kids at school, okay?" I nodded. "And you keep calling me. Okay? Bye. Bye now." And she hung up.

I could scarcely breathe from the still heat of the house. I opened a window but it didn't help. I found the control for the air conditioning and turned it down below sixty. I waited ten, fifteen, twenty minutes, all the time wishing my heart would stop going so fast, because the beats weren't just loud, they were exhausting me. The air didn't cool, nothing moved. I opened all the windows and poured myself a glass of water.

The closer I looked around the house now the more I saw the problems. They'd cut the baseboards out of short pieces, and hadn't forty-fived the joints, hadn't coped the corners, hadn't even set half the nails. The tape showed in the Sheetrock joints, the door margins weren't equal, the popcorn ceiling was discolored over the nails and at the seams. It was supposed to be better; it was so big, four bedrooms, with three full bathrooms, and a tray ceiling in the living room, tile on the bathroom walls. I could tell someone had thought they were buying a real decent house, but that wasn't what they got.

I couldn't believe my dad could stay in a house like that. There wasn't a single place you could look and see something done right. I went outside and stood away from it in the yard, with bunches of grass up to my knees, mosquitoes around my neck, gnats in my eyes, my ears. I'd never wanted to be so far away from a place. The pool liner had come apart at one corner. The narrow concrete path around it had stress fractures. I thought of my dad at some jobsite, probably looking at a hundred screw-ups that he'd have to fix, trying to figure out how to find decent carpenters, and do it all with hardly any money. I did wonder, there in that yard with the heat and the bugs, with that huge, hideous house looming over me, what it would take to make him snap. To feel like he had so many things go wrong, so many people giving him a hard time about everything, that he'd just have to take it out on someone.

I hit hard at the bugs, but all they did was swim away and come right back. "Goddamnit," I shouted to no one, "just stop stop stop." My clothes itched even where there were no bugs. I was supposed to wait for the movers. I was supposed to show them where to put things, even though I didn't know where things were supposed to go. I'd called my mom, like he said, but now was I supposed to tell him that she wasn't coming? Had she said for me to tell him that? How was I going to know what school I should go to, and how was I going to know other things, like who was going to fix dinner, or wash the clothes, or talk to my teachers? My dad would just do what he always did, work all the time, before I got up in the morning until seven or eight at night. And he'd get mad about everything.

I couldn't stand in the yard any longer and I couldn't bear to go into the house. I walked to the edge of the woods, right up to the underbrush. There was nowhere to get through it. Finally, down in a corner, I found a narrow break. The leaves and branches scraped me and I went in slowly, poking for snakes with a stick. I found clear places now, quiet places at first, with live oaks that dropped their limbs like they wanted me to come up. But I didn't want to climb, I wanted to keep going.

I wasn't alone. The voice that at first might have been nothing more than the buzzing of the gnats and mosquitoes grew louder and deeper as I went farther into the underbrush. I made out a few of the words but they were nothing, meaningless, a *this* or a *stop*. For a while I didn't even think it was aimed at me. It always came from about a dozen steps behind, close enough that for a while, when I'd turn, I figured whoever it was had just ducked behind a tree. The words rumbled like they came from a motorcycle at a stoplight. There was nothing dangerous or angry to them, even though they would not stop. Deeper into the brush I could barely move my legs through the tangled nets of branches and vines, and I'd long since quit even thinking of snakes.

More Like Not Running Away

"What?" I stopped, but when I turned around nothing moved. I waited. The words might have been important after all—I wished I had stopped sooner and actually listened. The way it came from far away but still brushed my ear, the lowness of it that I could hear in my bones, it could even have been God trying to tell me something again. "What?" I wasn't afraid, not really, except that I still couldn't make any sense of the words, and when I started walking again the voice was closer, then closer, and then I was running, the sharp branches and edges of the leaves cutting into my face and hands, some kind of animal darting out here and there ahead of me, and still the voice got closer, like it was trying to creep into my own head.

I smelled fire. I stopped, everything stopped, and I heard nothing now but tiny crackling way off. No way, I thought, these woods are on fire, they're burning, right over there, and when I turned around to run back I couldn't remember which way I'd come from. I'd never been lost, even though I'd walked all kinds of strange places in the woods, no matter how far I went or in what direction, I always came right back the same way, even without a path.

A hand, hard and soft in exactly the same places as my mom's, brushed the back of my neck. I turned around. No one. I listened again for the voice, afraid I would hear it, and afraid I wouldn't. "Who's there?" I asked, knowing when I said it that no one would answer. I rocked my head back and forth, but that didn't help.

I don't know what drove me to climb the tree, a live oak, with tremendous impossible limbs spread out like steps, but I had to get away, and the tree finally seemed like the only place to go. I climbed, but not like I had before. Now I kept slipping. In fact, a couple of times my foot missed a branch altogether and I had to catch myself. By the time I reached the top, I'd cut my hands and arms with the bark, and I wanted down right away. I stayed up long enough to see the fire, a strange one, in a long line, just tiny flames spreading from a swath of charred ground. The grass and brush were all burned behind the fire, but not the trees. I turned.

I couldn't see any houses, but I could see the way I'd come, the sandy patches, the three oaks, the clearings. At least I wasn't lost anymore. "Okay," I said. "I'll go," but the voice was gone. And I came down, waiting with each step for the voice, just knowing that if I heard it at the wrong time, I'd miss my step.

I've wondered why, when I'd heard so many things before, that particular voice scared me so much. I even thought I recognized it, but I couldn't name it. I know some of the reasons why this particular voice was a problem. It was real, for one, the way it always came from somewhere just behind me. Another thing is that it hurt, it somehow seemed to be so big, it pushed on my eardrums like I was deep under water. What I still think about, though, is how I couldn't stop it, how even when I rocked my head as hard as I could, I still had to listen.

"Controlled burns," my dad said. He came home from work not even dusty, but whistling, and brimming with new ideas. "They actually start them, little fires like that, so they don't get so many big ones." I was worried he'd see that I hadn't unpacked any boxes, not even made the beds, but he walked in with a bucket of fried chicken and a brand new boombox with a dozen cassettes. All that evening we listened to things I'd never heard before, classical music with long, low notes that sounded depressing at first, but then made me feel like someone's arms were warm around me.

The next night he brought home a pizza and a box full of

brand-new books, but these books weren't like the ones we had before. I'd read almost all of those, the shelf of *Reader's Digest Condensed Books*, *The Best Loved Poems of the American People*, *Bury My Heart at Wounded Knee*, the *Barnes & Noble Guide to Human Anatomy* that my dad once bought for me, so I could start learning to be a doctor, the *Stories of Love and Courage from Baptist Mission Fields* that my mom had borrowed from a church library in Colorado and never returned. I had never seen my dad reading these. He talked like reading was the most important thing me and Carson could do, but whenever he had a book in front of him, he hardly turned the pages, as though he was mired in the strings of words.

The books he took now from the top of the box were big, with hard covers that felt like cloth, with serious titles, *Material Methods*, *Industrial Standards and Measures*, *Properties of Concrete*, *Gypsum Primer*, *Management and the Critical Time Path Theory*. The paper was thick. Each page showed more detail, more layers of steel or rock or concrete, than I imagined would be used in a dozen buildings. The diagrams, calculations, numbered paragraphs, and drawings of cross sections made little sense but still I wondered at them, and I wondered if my dad did know how to read them.

The next morning he got up late. "Hey!" he said. "It's Sunday, you know. Let's get the hell out of here. Go see something. One of these sinks—I think they mean sinkholes—around here. What do you say?"

"Sure." I was more than ready to get out. I'd already decided I wasn't going to start at a new school—I couldn't imagine all those kids and teachers moving all the time, talking, slamming their books. But even with the couple of walks I'd taken, after two days the house had started to close in on me.

When we got outside I saw he had a new truck. It had to be brand new, a steel-gray Chevy Silverado with a diamondplate chrome toolbox across the bed. Other than that, it was just a truck, not a jacked-up four-wheel drive, no whip antennas, no decals, just a lean pickup that looked ready to work.

He didn't say anything, he just unlocked the doors. Inside, the only thing special besides the new, slightly cigarette smell were the mud mats, with their deep soft rubber grooves.

"So," he said, "here we go." He slid the gearshift into drive and we took off, a smooth, hungry acceleration. "I'm thinking the ocean," he said, "it's been a long time since I saw that." He could hardly contain the satisfaction in his voice.

"You know," he said, lighting a cigarette and taking an easy breath, "I've been thinking. That house, you know, in Michigan. Maybe that was the best thing that could have happened. I'm looking at more money right now than I ever dreamed I'd make. The guys who own this development, don't get me wrong, they're a bunch of rip-off artists every bit as much as anyone else, but they believe in one thing: paying enough so they don't have to worry about something getting done. They got jobs in Pensacola, Jacksonville, Panama City, all over the place, and I'm going to be putting out bids with them, and with some other companies, to subcontract the rough carpentry. They sure as hell could use someone who knows how to run a framing crew. These last guys, Jesus Christ, they'd framed an entire building with untreated lumber on the bottom plates. Can you imagine that?" I could see his teeth. "There's not a damn thing you can do except tear every wall apart and start over."

We weren't driving anywhere in particular, just turning from one dirt road to another, the rear wheels plowing into the sandy shoulders. Gentle clouds of dust rolled out behind us. "So anyway," I said, "I've been thinking, Dad. About the house here, you know? Just listen a minute and tell me what you think. I know we just moved and all, but what if we, if you and me, today even, drove around for a while to see if we couldn't find something, I don't know, a place that didn't need so much work? I mean, I think maybe Mom would like to have a place maybe in town, with just a neat little yard, where we could walk places."

I could always tell by the way he smoked what kinds of thoughts he was having, and right then he exhaled in a perfect, gentle stream. It was a good time to talk about things. I thought for just a minute that I might tell him about what my mom had said, that she might be staying in Seattle a while, but I decided to wait. I could tell he was in the kind of good mood that could turn bad pretty quick. Besides, my mom hadn't really said she wasn't coming back. She'd just said that it would be a little while.

"Sure," he said. "We could live anywhere. That's what I meant, about losing that house. Anywhere," he said again, looking a long time out his side window. "That's why I'm doing all this, starting this subcontracting business myself. That's just the beginning. I want to start building high-end custom homes, nothing but top of the line. And condos, these guys I'm with now are talking high-dollar communities outside Washington DC. They've got framing subcontracts they need filled in Virginia, Maryland. This thing could go all up and down the East Coast. They've got serious money behind them. There's more money in this than we'll ever need. It's just waiting. It's going to happen."

I recognized the hard excitement in my chest. I wanted to ask all the right questions, to keep him talking, but when I swallowed, the words stuck.

"I'm telling you," he said, his voice getting tighter, "after dealing with that son of a bitch banker up in Michigan, listening to his lilywhite bullshit about contracts and completion schedules, I don't care if I've got to make ten million dollars. Not a man on this earth is ever going to put my family through that again." He clenched the steering wheel. "Never," he said quietly.

Then, like he'd heard a voice somewhere, he suddenly relaxed again, like he'd been only a few moments before, and shook his head, clearing it. "There I go again," he laughed, "now where were we." He stared at a point through the windshield. "As a matter of fact, where in the hell are we?"

We'd turned down so many roads. I was excited thinking about having so much money, even if it wasn't exactly like he'd said it would be, it might be enough for a house.

"I don't care," he said, raising his hands off the steering wheel. "What the hell does it matter where we're at? See, that's what I'm saying. Why do we always have to be going *somewhere*? Today, just for once let's try not going anywhere. And just see. Where we wind up."

Then the road we were on ended, just like that, without even a sign, and we could see a thin line of woods, and between the trees, blue-gray water. We only had to walk a minute, and there we were, standing in reedy grass up to our thighs, right at the ocean. It lapped into the grass at our feet, and everywhere the sun lit up little waves of it.

"You knew just where we were, didn't you?" I asked.

"Rough idea," he said. "Something about the ocean. Keep your ears open, and you'll always get there." He held one arm straight out over the water. "Ain't it something, though," he said, "just huge, and like this one minute, as quiet as anything else. Then the next minute, it can be—"

More Like Not Running Away

Once, he told me about driving to the beach with his best friend, Har Lee Pendergraft, both of them mad drunk, Har Lee at the wheel and blindfolded, my dad directing him, saying an inch to the right, an inch to the left. I thought now he might tell me that story again, or about when he was a lifeguard at Wrightsville Beach, just before he ran away from home, when a guy who drowned swallowed his tongue, so my dad had to safety-pin it to the inside of his cheek so he could breathe again. But he didn't talk about any of that, as a matter of fact he didn't talk about anything for the longest time. He just stood like he'd lost something out in the water.

"Well," he said very softly, just like the little waves, "it has a way of putting you in your place, doesn't it? I mean, think about how much damage this ocean can do. How many thousands of people it's killed. Families tore apart, buildings and ships, all destroyed. But you can't hate it, can you? Never a regret. And people just keep coming back.

"I used to think about being an artist. Did I ever tell you that? When I was a lifeguard I used to look out over that ocean and just dream and dream." He looked down at his hard fingernails, at the sandy skin of his hands. "I had a teacher tell me once that I saw things like nobody else. I'll never forget that. Not too many people in Laurinburg had much good to say to me then. But she was right, I always saw my own colors."

I wanted to listen forever. The air off the ocean, warm and light and salty on my tongue, surrounded me like I was actually in the water, and it was taking me, down and away.

The day he'd let me steer seemed like so many years ago. Something I forgot about that day, what he did say—I wasn't sure about it before, but every time I was about to run into something, when I'd get too close to a tree or too near to a hole, he'd touch the steering wheel and say Easy, cheetah. What I liked was how he would call me a cheetah, and even then I knew the best part about cheetahs was that they were easy, they could run sixty miles an hour and their feet hardly touched the ground. I don't know who I was talking to, but I said it then, at the beach, just to myself: Easy, cheetah.

That night we started reading the books he'd brought home. I took out a biography of someone I'd never heard of, John Roebling, who designed the Brooklyn Bridge. By the time I'd finish a sentence, I couldn't remember what it said in the beginning, but I didn't mind. I just let my eyes skip over the words. I didn't care about the book, even though I kept to it. What mattered was that my dad was in the room, reading about important things. The light from the lamp over his head, the lazy curls of cigarette smoke, the way he ground his thumb into his chin—I wanted it to last as long as it could. After a while I put some coffee in the percolator, then brought us each a cup. For the first time, I wanted a cigarette, not to watch the smoke or to hold it cool in my fingers, but because of hunger. I didn't get one, though. I didn't want to break the mood.

"You know what this is?" He started to mouth a word, but didn't; he just turned his book enough for me to see his forefinger resting under a word.

I got up and went over. "Brisance?" I wanted desperately to know right then, to be able to say it as I was walking back to my chair, to give him something just that easily, but of course I didn't know what it meant. I went downstairs to the moving box marked *books* and found the dictionary, and found the word. "It means the shattering or crushing of an explosive," I said. I lay the dictionary on the table beside where I was sitting, and twice more that night, I heard the tapping of his finger against the page, and I went over to see the word, and looked it up, and told him what it meant. Then he fell asleep in the chair, with the book on his chest, and I finally had my cigarette. I began, then, to follow the biography of John Roebling, and I can say to this day exactly what kind of a man he was, what his fears were, and why he wanted to build that bridge, when so many people told him not to.

D uval swings around the steeple to talk to me. *"There's a rumor,"* he says, *"that a guy named Tenzing actually carried Hillary to the summit. Of Everest. Bet you never heard of a Tenzing."*

I think he's joking, that he's going to say something like a Tenzing is kind of rope, but he's serious. "He's a Sherpa, he was up there with Hillary, but nobody talks about him. He wrote a book, but he wouldn't say who was actually the first one up there."

Duval says he's aiming to climb Everest four years from now. "I'm young, I can train plenty by then," he says. "And it's not like you go it alone, you know. You hire a guide, somebody who's been there, knows the ropes," he laughs, "and you're with a group of people. Doctors go up there, lawyers, women too.

"Don't get me wrong. It's still dangerous. They say it's not the hardest mountain to climb, but it's easy to get killed. Storms, blizzards come out of nowhere. And the breathing, the thin air, that kills people. Some people can take it, some can't."

I've always missed this: I'd always pictured somebody who climbed a mountain doing it alone, carrying everything on his own back. That's how I'd pictured Sir Edmund Hillary, when all I knew was that he'd been the first person to climb Everest, that he stood up there, one man, on top of the world. And when Duval told me about Tenzing, and all the work the Sherpas did, that all changed.

Duval's going to do it, I know. And I bet the people he goes with, even if they don't all get to the top, are going to say that when they were there, they were glad to have Duval with them. He's like that. Sometimes when we're on a steeple, when we've been working right next to each other ten or eleven hours at a stretch, I just don't want to come down.

Everything Waits

I BEGAN TO THINK THAT ME AND MY DAD might stay after all. Over the next two weeks we read more and more in the evenings, and whenever we talked, we talked softly, like we had a new language. He had the same, warm voice he'd had that day at the beach. I unpacked some of the boxes, got out some dishes and pots, and enough clothes for me and him. I left the rest packed. I figured out the washing machine, and when he undressed at night I'd get his clothes, wash and dry them, and put them away. He brought home boxes of macaroni and cheese, frozen dinners, cereal, soap, detergents, and I put them away. I started cleaning the house even though he never said anything about it, wiping out drawers, mopping the floors, even scrubbing the toilets and the dark grout in the showers. I found a phone book and called an exterminator and someone to come clean out the pool.

The quiet in the house grew, and at first I liked it. I plugged

More Like Not Running Away

Carson's radio in my room and left it on all day. The music it played was the same music Carson used to listen to, rock songs that pretty soon all sounded the same, with drums and guitars and people singing. After a while I learned a few of the tunes and would nod with them. When I heard my dad coming down the driveway, I'd turn it off. I walked in the woods some more, looking for another fire, but all I saw were places like caves made of vines and twisted branches.

The way the woods were dark made me realize that I wouldn't have liked to work on the Brooklyn Bridge. The guys had to go down under water into these places called caissons. I'd never seen one, but I figured they must have been dark, and wet. What they didn't know when they built the bridge was that underwater there was too much pressure, it could actually kill the men building it. And it did—at least three died from it.

I missed my mom more than I thought I would. I could have called her, but I didn't know what I'd say. My dad didn't ask anything about her. I went into the bedroom where her boxes were, and opened one to put her clothes away. I picked up one of her shirts, but I couldn't, I put it back. I didn't realize then that I was waiting for the phone to ring, but most of the day, each day, that's what made the quiet stick in my throat.

"I want you to call your mother today." He stood at the foot of my bed. I was just waking up, and pulled the covers over my body. "It's been three weeks. Enough. I'm wiring her five thousand dollars this afternoon. Tell her to get her and Carson a plane ticket, and pay off whatever she needs to in Seattle. I want her home." He turned and left, the edges of his voice still ringing from the walls. A few minutes later his truck spun down the driveway.

I knew he was making money. Not just the hundreds he left

on the dresser. He had told me that over the next few months he was going to be bringing in enough to buy the house we were in if we wanted, with a quarter of the money in cash. I saw checks for ten, fifteen thousand dollars made out to Lever Contracting.

I had thought about talking to him, seeing if he had enough money to pay for what he'd done to the house in Michigan. I still worried every time I heard a car go by our house that it would be someone coming to arrest him, or serve papers, or whatever they would do to make him pay for it. Little details of what he'd done kept coming back to me—the ripped up pipes and wiring, the gashes in every piece of Sheetrock—and I realized how much it would take to put things back together. But I didn't say anything to him. I told myself that what he needed, what we needed, was for him to have some time to get his head together. And now, if my mom would come back like he wanted, whatever problem he'd left in Michigan, the money could fix.

I turned on the radio. So I was going to call her after all. And she would be coming back, I guessed. I got in the shower, but I heard him call me, so I wrapped a towel around my waist and went into the hallway, but he wasn't there. I looked out the window—his truck was still gone. That scared me a little. I rinsed off and went to the kitchen to call my mom right then—I had to hear her voice. A real voice, not a radio one, not one from the bones of the house.

"Oh, honey, it's you." The familiar, scratchy breath touched like a fingertip at the edge of my ear. I moved the phone and pulled the towel tighter around my waist.

"Frankie?" I didn't say her name loud enough, and part of it caught in my throat. "How are you?"

"Fine ... is this ... Levi?" It was her old voice now, the one she used with me and Carson. "Is that really you?"

More Like Not Running Away

"Yes."

"Your voice is deeper! Did you know that? Is it changing? I'll bet you're as tall as your mom, aren't you?"

"I don't know," I said. Frankie was right, I had noticed the last few days that my voice would break every now and then. And now, when I looked down, I thought I could see a couple of hairs that were different, more like real hairs.

She whispered, "do you have a girlfriend there yet? Is that okay to ask?"

"I don't." I laughed a little, it felt good. I thought about saying wait a second and going to my room to put on underwear. "Is my mom there?"

She clicked her tongue. "Well, you know what? She's just so into things. She's here one minute and gone the next. Those articles—have you read those? Well let me tell you, Sport, she's got a little talent for that stuff. I actually heard someone talking about one of them the other day, some guy in a coffee shop here, saying, *Did you read the one about people who shortchain their dogs?* She wrote about that, you know, about how people should have to be chained to their own doghouses. Anyway, what I mean is she's not here right now. Should I have her call you?"

Cool air ran down my back. I mumbled no.

Frankie cleared her throat. "Levi, honey, remember what you told me last time I saw you? You were up on that roof preaching, and we were downstairs talking about you. We were saying, even your teachers always said, we just couldn't think of a finer boy."

There was a loose Pall Mall on the counter. I reached for it, and the towel came off.

"I think your mom's worried about you down there. How much longer will you be in school, before summer vacation?"

I found a book of matches and lit the cigarette. The fresh taste soothed my stomach. I lay down on the linoleum floor and then sat up again to look for an ashtray, but there wasn't one within reach. "In a little while," I said. "I think my dad wants her to come home. He told me to call her to say he's wiring her some money, and she's supposed to fly home, and she's supposed to get Carson a ticket too."

For a while Frankie didn't answer. Finally, she said, "I think she does need to call you, honey. I thought she'd told you—"

"This is such a weird place, Aunt Frankie," I said, "sometimes I look around at things in this house and it's like someone else is living here, someone I'm supposed to know. But I don't."

"Maybe you're just homesick, honey."

"But I'm home," I said. "How can I be homesick at home?"

I thought she'd laugh, but she didn't. I lay back down and gently tapped the ashes to my bare stomach. They burned only for a split second. I touched the fire from the tip of the cigarette to my wrist and jerked it back. It left a faint burn.

"Aunt Frankie, when you ran away from home how'd you know where to go?"

"That was so long ago. Let me think—I guess I knew somebody in California who said I could stay with them. That's right—Jeannie Ensing. She was sweet. I should call her sometime."

"Why did you run away?"

She was rubbing the phone on her ear. "Well that's a long story. Nothing horrible was happening, if that's what you're wondering. Mainly, nothing was happening. But listen, I hope you're not thinking—"

"Not really. I don't know anybody in California anyway. I don't really know anybody, like that I could go live with."

More Like Not Running Away

A car pulled into our driveway. "Someone's here," I said hurriedly. I pulled myself up, but the fire from the cigarette brushed the inside of my leg, just above the knee. When I jerked the cigarette back, it went from my hand on to a chair cushion, then rolled down into a crack. A tiny wisp of smoke drifted up. I dropped the phone, and tried to reach into the crack for the cigarette. It burned me. I dropped it again, then I finally reached in and grabbed it, fire and all, and ran to the sink. I filled a glass of water, and ran back to the chair, and poured it in the hole the cigarette had burned.

Frankie's voice called out small from the phone on the floor. I picked it up. "Okay," I said, "okay."

"Levi! What happened? What was all that?"

"It's okay," I said, "just an accident. Something fell."

She waited, then laughed a little. "Did it fall up?" she said. "You know, like you told me, always fall up? Did it fall up?"

"Not really." I looked around for my towel. The front door opened. "I have to go," I said.

"Okay," she said. "But listen, one thing, honey." I couldn't find the towel, and I wanted to hang up so I could go. "When you talk to your mom, you know, this has been hard on her."

"I really should go now," I said, stretching the phone cord, looking under the table for the towel.

"Okay," Frankie said, "just listen, whatever she says, none of this is your fault."

"Okay," I said, "I'm listening."

"What in the hell are you doing?" My dad looked at some point behind me. "Where in the hell are your clothes?"

I still held the phone. I tried to cover myself with my other hand as I slid around him to the steps. "I was in the bathroom," I said, "I had to get the phone."

"Well get some goddamn clothes on," he said. "I need you to come with me for a minute."

He was finishing a cigarette by the time I climbed in the truck next to him. When the truck started moving, I realized how much I'd been wanting to ride, anywhere, again. Tufts of Spanish moss, hanging from the live oaks, broke the sunlight on the road into small shadows.

"You call her?"

The road behind us ran up the sideview mirror. "She wasn't there."

"Hm." And that was it—I recognized it at last—the voice that followed me in the woods was his voice. Dark, distant, with words too bitter to speak out loud. His voice, even then, even as I nodded my head, drove right up to my eardrums. He knew somehow that I hadn't talked to my mom because she was gone somewhere, and he knew the person that I had been talking to was probably Frankie, and I could tell by the cutting of his eyes that all this was adding up to something he didn't like.

"My family," he said, "is not going to end this way. Living in mobile homes or condos or whatever. I know what's going on. I know." He laughed unhappily. "That banker, that twerp at the bank up there. It'd be worth it to me sometime to see him choke on his own medicine. Buy every house on his street and let them rot, watch him scramble while his property value goes to hell. Money, that's the only thing little shits like that understand."

He'd talked that way before, but now was different. I didn't like to hear him go on about it. I thought the guy at the bank was probably, like my mom said, just some peon who didn't really make the decisions. "Maybe it wasn't all his fault," I said. "Maybe he just had to do it, you know?"

More Like Not Running Away

I could tell it was the wrong thing to say before I finished talking. He didn't say anything back, but his face clouded and he started saying things under his breath.

It was then that I started thinking about what I'd do, if he did take off after someone. I played it different ways, throwing myself at him to stop him, actually trying to fight him, my fists coming loose against his chest, making him say he was sorry. None of it seemed very real, it was more like watching it happen on television, but I knew one thing: I'd be there.

We ended up at the jobsite. It was quiet; no compressors, no generators, no Skilsaws, no hammers. We walked along the sandy unpaved main street, past a half dozen cul-de-sacs that were partly cleared. Most of the houses we came to first were still only foundations, or even stakes. The houses would be small ones, close together, with garages that opened right into the street. Whole units of studs were split and warped, bundles of plywood gouged by forklifts.

He took me out of the sun into an air-conditioned trailer. "All right, then," he said finally, "here's what I need you to do. See these numbers?" He pointed to a messy stack of papers on a desk made from a sheet of plywood over sawhorses. "Call these people and tell them I said that we're running a week behind right now. You understand?"

There were about twenty pieces of paper, some with more than one phone number. "Are these subcontractors? What if they want to ask something?"

He slid a couple of the papers around with his forefinger. "Yeah," he said, "some of them are. Or suppliers. I don't want anything delivered on time either. Everything waits a week."

"Will you be around?"

"You bet," he said. "Just stay in here." He left.

I shoved his old coffee cups and full ashtrays to one side, then called the first number. "Hello?" a woman said. I hadn't expected a woman to answer.

"Hello? Is this—" I couldn't think of who I'd called.

She acted like I was supposed to say something then. "What is it, kid?" she said finally. The words my dad had just said, something about waiting a week, were suddenly lost in dozens of other words.

"I don't know," I said. "I'm sorry. I was supposed to call you about something."

"Who are you?"

I mumbled my name back to her, too soft, I knew, for her to hear.

"Well jeez, kid. I'm busy here, you know," she said, and then the phone just buzzed in my ear. Her voice, the pieces of her words, kept playing over and over in my head.

My dad's truck engine started. I couldn't remember—had he said for me to come outside? I stepped out of the trailer. He drove away, past a few of the houses, then stopped, nose-to-nose to an old panel van. He reached behind the front seat and pulled out his leather toolbelt, cinched it around his waist. He fished through a gangbox in the back of the truck like he was ripping it apart, pulling out handfuls of sixteen penny sinkers, a twenty-five-foot Stanley tape, a square, a chalkbox, red and blue lumber crayons. One at a time he jammed them into the belt. They fell in easily, taking their old shapes in the leather. Finally he took out his thirty-two ounce corrugated-head framing hammer, the hammer I still could not swing right, the hammer I'd heard carpenter after carpenter say they didn't believe a man could use. He dropped it into the holster. He threw an orange drop cord and a wormdrive Skilsaw to the ground.

More Like Not Running Away

A fat man and a couple of other guys came around the side of one of the houses. I realized something wasn't right, and I ducked down, then sneaked into one of the partly framed houses. Please, I prayed, please just turn around. The men walked around the panel van. They looked like they were waiting for my dad to leave so they could finish telling a joke.

"Country." My dad waved the fat man toward him.

"Sure, boss." He came over, looking crosswise to my dad with a sour expression.

"You're off the job. I don't want no trouble, just take your boys and get."

The fat man sniffed. "Bullshit I am," he said with a voice that sounded like he was talking through a wet pipe.

I quit breathing and stood perfectly still. There were four men, including Country. They must have been the ones making everything a week late, so now plumbers couldn't run pipes because the walls were set wrong, electricians had probably showed up to run wire and turned around and left, because the walls weren't done. I saw now where beer cans dotted the ditches and brush at the edge of the job. I'd heard all my life about that kind of construction crew. Tools were probably disappearing.

Three more men came around from another house.

"Think," my dad said softly. He stood like he was straining against an invisible chain. For a second, I thought he was talking to me.

The men formed a semicircle, their muscles tight, their eyes on my dad. One of them picked up a crowbar lying on a nearby box, and others touched their Buck knife cases. They didn't talk.

When my dad started to take his framing hammer out the holster, I was sure that was it, he was going to start swinging it.

I walked out, toward him. There was trash everywhere—two-by-four blocks, steel lumber straps—the ground was sandy, I could hardly keep from tripping or sliding. Every step got heavier. Still, I came to the men, not looking, and they made no sounds. I went right next to my dad's hammer. I tried to stand straight but my breaths were so short, I knew I was shaking.

"Go back to the trailer." My dad put his arm over my chest, pushing me.

"I called," my voice was so high. "But they're not, they didn't—" I gave up.

"I said go on. Now."

I stayed. "Can we go? I have to get home. I'm feeling kind of sick I think."

He moved his hand again on the hammer, and I went to grab it, to stop him. His forearm was huge in my hand, and I realized that I couldn't hold it at all. I tried, awkwardly, to pull his hand from the hammer, but he took me by the collar, almost gently. He pushed me away, gently too, but my legs were soft under me and I went down to the ground.

"Go on. I'll be right there. Don't make me say it again."

I got up, and started toward his truck. My legs kept shaking even after I sat down and put my hands on them. I could still see and hear the men.

"I'd think twice if I were any of you," my dad said evenly, his black eyes moving from man to man. "If you're able to think twice, that is." I could tell from how the men sunk away, only a few inches, not even stepping back, but just out of his reach, they saw it. Country's smirk twitched away, and the semicircle loosened.

The men blinked, murmured. "You owe us for two weeks," Country said.

My dad moved toward me, but easily. He reached in the

cab of the truck, pulled out the company checkbook. He wrote it right on the hood, and the men did not watch. When Country reached out to take it, I finally swallowed.

I could still taste it in the air. I read once that soldiers know that taste, like a dull knife on the crease of their tongues, just before things start going wrong.

My dad came straight back to the truck. He threw his toolbelt to the floor by my feet.

"Those guys," he said, "you just about got to slap them in the face before you start talking, so they know which way to listen." I nodded. "Let's just get out of here," he said. "Let's just get the hell out of here."

He started the engine with his foot to the floor. It wound all the way up and shuddered through the seat. He ripped the gearshift all the way down, then up, yanking it so hard that something broke. When it finally went into reverse, it hung wrong, and he slammed his foot to the floor again. We flew backwards, barely missing a couple of trees, throwing roostertails of sand as far as the front doors of the houses. Something crunched, then slid. The door next to me swiped against a tree. He backed up and took off again, right over two-by-fours, the back end fishtailing wildly and jumping over ditches. My side mirror hung by a single screw.

He didn't slow down when he turned out of the jobsite. The tail end skidded sideways down the sand shoulder for a bit, then he put his foot to the floor again and steered out of it. All I saw were blurred trees and dust clouds out the back.

I needed to take a leak by now, and when I turned to the window, my neck hurt. I was so mad that my hands were pure white and wouldn't move. Even as we kept going faster, everything outside seemed to slow down and lose color.

We came to an intersection where he couldn't see. He had to stop, but he almost didn't. A crossing car laid on the horn, swerving wide around us. He slammed his fist into the dashboard, leaving a baseball-sized dent in the vinyl. "Son of a bitch," he said. "Tell me what she said." His voice was suddenly calm.

I had no idea where we were. There were no buildings in sight. Then I got out. "I'm going home." I'd walked only a dozen feet from the back of the truck when I heard his door open.

"Just a minute," he said.

"I'm not getting in," I said. "You're going to kill us. You're going to kill me."

"You can't walk from here. You don't know, I don't even know where we are." His voice was drained.

I left anyway. The engine fired just as I crossed in front of the truck, and for that instant I thought that even if I wasn't afraid, I should be. But the truck didn't move. I walked away, and walked for hours, then finally down the sandy shoulder of Sopchoppy's main street, past the abandoned stores and lots, where stores once stood or never stood, where patches of weeds grew, and in the open and heavy air I wondered if I would ever go home. The places in and around Sopchoppy were never any different from the places I had seen before, but now I longed to know what was inside any one of the houses. I looked into windows. But even when I saw a face, it did not give anything away. A pale barber, a little girl pulling away from her mother. Nothing. I wandered hour after hour. I felt the dreaming and tiredness of Sopchoppy, and I could not rest for it.

We Seen You Fall

FOR THE NEXT TWO WEEKS A SHARP SILENCE took over. The grass grew, but we didn't have a lawnmower and I didn't want to call anyone about it. I hadn't even been in the pool before the water turned green. I thought my dad might notice that things were starting to look worse, but most of the time when he came home he just ate and went to bed, without saying anything.

I heard things all the time now. One day when I was walking in the woods, a soft rain started when I was still a long way from home. The drops fell from my hair to my cheeks over and over. Pretty soon the wet brush soaked my pants and boots. I thought about not going home at all, just walking until the woods ended, then walking some more into a town and through that town until I could find an open church and sleep on a pew, until some preacher would wander in and find me and take me home. My clothes were scratching me so hard, they hurt.

More Like Not Running Away

I wondered if I should say something to my dad that night when he came home, that we couldn't stay in the house anymore. I imagined that I was aiming a heavy pistol at him while I talked, and made him stay away from me while I told him everything—how Mom would not come home because he lied, because when he got mad, his eyes were steel bits spinning into our bones.

But I came home like always. The phone was ringing as I walked through the yard, through the house. It rang twenty times at least.

"Levi," he said, his voice cutting soft. "I need you to bring me something."

"Where are you?"

"I'm at Tallahassee Memorial Hospital in room 241."

"What happened?" I shivered in my damp clothes.

"I fell. I cut my thumb off."

"Wha—you cut it off? On purpose?" I took off my shirt.

"Jesus Christ, of course not. I was standing on a ladder, and I slipped. The Skilsaw came down on me. But listen, I'll tell you about it later. I want you to get me some clothes—pants, shirt, underwear, and I mean something decent. My khakis, a dress shirt, and my Florsheim shoes. And my razor—are you writing this down?"

I started. "Just a minute," I said, and I dug a carpenter's pencil and a scrap paper out of a drawer.

"My razor, shaving cream, deodorant, all that. You got it? Okay, then call a cab. You'll need money. There's money in the top drawer of my dresser. Get a hundred, at least. And for God's sake, hold on to it."

"How do I get a cab?"

"Call one. Listen now. One more thing. Don't call your mother. I mean it. If she calls, don't talk to her. If anyone calls, just hang up, just get down here right away. You understand? Don't talk to anyone."

I couldn't name what was scaring me so much, but my hands would not stop shaking. Maybe, I thought, he was hurt worse than he said, or he'd done something terrible, that it wasn't a saw at all. The cabdriver tried to talk to me, but his voice came from so far away that I couldn't keep his words strung together.

When I got to the hospital, the woman at the desk looked behind me to see if an adult was with me. I told her I had my dad's stuff and she let me in. Walking down those wide, white hallways, making turn after turn, past all the dark offices, past whispering nurses and people's soft-spoken rooms, the machinery of the hospital itself—the great pumps, the electricity, the pressure of the oxygen—began drowning out everything else. By the time I got to my dad's room, I was shaking so hard that I had to stop outside his door and hold my head between my hands before I could go in.

He lay heavily in the white bed and he still smelled of smoke and sawdust, but also of antiseptic. He was asleep, his square, dark face unrelaxed, his jaw still clenched, his eyebrows drawn together, even his shoulders held back. It took me a few minutes to figure out what was so different about how he looked, until I realized how white his skin was. He breathed like the air in the room might have some poison to it.

He turned a bit, and I saw the hand, wrapped in a mitten of white bandages, laid gently on his chest. There was still sawdust in the creases of his neck. I thought about stirring him, even though I knew that he always woke up violently, his eyes wide and his voice going full strength, yelling to know what had happened. A few hours passed, midnight came, and I realized that I hadn't eaten since breakfast that morning. The hunger, once I recognized it, would not stay put, but kept reaching up, like it had sharp fingers. I went to the cafeteria and bought a ready-made sandwich and ate it, then another, then another. I got a cup of coffee and went back to his room. For five more hours I waited in the darkness while he slept, and I didn't think of anything except that darkness. I studied his face in a way I'd never been able to before, so that after a while I knew the line of his whiskers, the movements of his mouth.

"Hey," he said at last. It was six in the morning. His lips were colorless. "Get me a drink of water, will you?" He drank desperately, set the glass down, and sat up in the bed. "Okay," he said, "It's okay." He raised his eyes gently like an old man. "I'm sorry. Sorry about how I've been. I should've gone to church, I guess, said my prayers. I should've never turned the tables over. I had this coming to me. I sure have been a son of a bitch, huh?" He shook his head. "Well, I'll make it up, to everybody. Then what?" He closed his eyes like he'd drift off again.

Then he sat, wide awake, "I've got to talk to your mother. I want you to pack us. Our best clothes, a couple of weeks' worth. Wash whatever needs to be washed. Today."

I pointed to his bandaged hand. "What happened?"

He lifted it. "We'll talk later. I'm tired. Just get on home, like I said, and pack our shit. I'll be there later today. This doctor's supposed to come by at lunch. I got to talk to him before I leave."

People in the halls were talking, people in other rooms were talking, the machinery of the hospital kept right on going. "Where? Why are we leaving? Where are we going?"

He waved me away. "Just be ready when I get home."

On the way home, I asked the cabdriver to leave me at the Maverick convenience store in Sopchoppy. The only person there was a girl, a teenager, behind the counter who was reading a magazine.

"I'd like a pack of Pall Malls," I said.

She reached under the counter and pulled out an open pack of Benson & Hedges Menthol 100's and a small pink and white ashtray. "Here," she said. "You're kind of young to be buying cigarettes, aren't you? I'm not supposed to give cigarettes to kids." She lit one herself. The blue smoke came up from her like a private cloud. She was not beautiful. Her auburn hair lay too flat to her head. She was dressed in chemical colors, and the clothes looked hot and itchy on her skin.

I took one of the cigarettes.

"So." She looked out the door for a car or another person, then held out the lighter. "You take that cab here?"

I nodded. There was pink lipstick on the filter of her cigarette.

"School out for summer already?"

I wanted to leave, and I wanted to stay. "My dad's in the hospital," I said. "He fell off a ladder and cut his thumb off."

She whistled. "You're kidding. Is he . . . okay?"

"They sewed it back on. I didn't see it."

"Sounds gross. A guy around here got killed once cause a bullet came down on him. Somebody shot up in the air, and it came down." She leaned across the counter. The menthol made her breath sweet. "Course it couldn't of landed on my old man, that would of been an act of God."

She leaned closer. "You look familiar, your eyes do. You know what they look like? I'm trying to think."

"Like broken glass. Anyway that's what somebody told me once." I couldn't look at her. And I couldn't turn away.

"That's not what I was thinking," she said. "But now I am. It's true. They look kind of dangerous, you know?"

"No." I didn't think she was kidding or being mean, but I wasn't sure.

Then she came out from behind the counter, sniffing around the coffee machine, the hot dog rack. "Something's burning," she said. Then she went outside. I followed her, not knowing what I should do. She walked around back. When I got there, she was pointing to the woods behind the store. A long gray cloud of smoke billowed up from a ways off.

"Controlled burns, right?" I said.

She stepped right next to me. "Like I know. Nice shirt." She slipped her fingertips between the buttons over my stomach. The slight scratch of her nails electrified a single nerve running from my navel to my crotch. I wasn't sure if she was actually moving her finger, or it only felt that way. She pulled her hand out of my shirt. One of her nails caught the hard denim at the waist of my jeans. "Oh God," she said, like she might cry. The air around us was so heavy, so still, my breath kept catching.

She pushed my head back and looked into my eyes. "Broken glass. Kind of pretty, you know. You should be careful about that."

A car pulled into the parking lot out front. "I got to go now," she said. "But come back if you want another smoke."

Even when I couldn't see her anymore, my skin ached just where her finger had been. I needed to pee, but I didn't think I could right then, I had to go too bad. I followed a street that I didn't know, except it did seem to go in the general direction of our house. It also went toward the fire.

When I couldn't see buildings anymore, I walked into the woods, following the smoke. I got to where I could actually see the faraway licks of flames. I circled wide around to where the ground was black and smoldering, but the leaves were still damp underneath.

Within thirty feet of the fire, the ground got hot. The flames were small, licking at the bottom of the bushes, like they were asking permission to climb up. I could taste the smoke, and it left sprinkles of ashes on my arms. I walked a perimeter. The terrain changed a bit, rolled some, and around a break the flames grew to about four feet high and I cut a wider berth. It was more fire than I'd ever seen and I wanted to see all of it if I could. It had a quiet crackling to it that I craved. But it did get hotter, and I could see now where it had taken out smaller trees too.

All of a sudden the wind changed and I was breathing ashy smoke and had to turn away. I knew that I was heading away from the fire itself and onto cooler ground, but the wind kept at my back with the soot and black and heat. The woods here were thick, too thick for much light to get through. I could just feel the snakes running from the fire to the wet air. I was in brush, just to my knees, and I stopped. I could breathe now. My shirt was gray with ashes, so I took it off and shook it out. The skin on my stomach, where the girl had touched me, was white, the muscles small.

I couldn't hold it anymore. I pulled down my jeans to take a leak. The heat from the ground felt so good. I thought of the girl's hand.

It stung, between my legs. And then it stung again, on both legs and my ankles and then my groin. I looked at the ashes on my boots; something moved. Fire ants. I saw them in a rough line coming up my left leg, and along my groin, to my stomach. I started swatting hard at them, knocking them from my thigh, and my pants fell the rest of the way down to my ankles and I saw dozens of them and they bit and bit until my skin burned. My boot was in the ant mound. I leaned over and swatted but they had crawled all in my socks and boots and I jerked my foot from the mound and started to pull off the boots but the strings wouldn't come undone. I yanked hard. My leg came against a dead branch and I lost my balance and fell to the ground, thinking just before I hit that I was always supposed to know which way to fall, but I hadn't known I was going to fall, so I hadn't thought about the best way down. In a split of light, I cracked my head against a rock. A small thought flickered—did I cry when I killed the cat with the kittens still inside her? But my eyes would not stay open.

"Jesus Christ, kid. You're lucky to be alive here." The voice came from behind my head. I couldn't turn to see who it was.

"You need some help," another man said. "Can you stand up?"

I looked behind me enough to see their black fireboots. I started to say something, but pinpricks of heat, like bee stings at first, started everywhere along my skin at the same time, then spread, hotter and hotter, so I could barely move. I held a hand up to my eyes; red welts covered it, went up the inside of my forearm, trailing in a zagged line from around my armpit to my chest. I was naked. I could only get a short breath down, and I tried to cover myself with my hand but I didn't want to touch myself.

"Um, we got your clothes right here, kid." The first man pointed to my clothes hanging from a tree branch. He was turned away from me. My skin was so white, and the welts were so red. I grabbed my clothes and put them on. "When we got here you was covered all up with them ants, they was all in you, all in your clothes and stuff. They about chewed you to the bone. We had to, you see, take off these clothes to get them ants off of you. They was in your boots, everywhere."

The other man looked at his hands. They were both heavyset, with thick beards. "We was out here watching over the fires," the other man said, "and saw you walking around the burn. You shouldn't of been here. You might ought to go on to a doctor."

Their voices sawed. I couldn't make out all the words through the heat in my head.

"I was just," I said, "I was just trying to run away—"

"Kid," one of the men said, "You got somebody at home to look after you?"

I nodded. "My mom is home," I said. I caught my breath. "Did you—"

"We seen you fall kid," one of the men said. "We seen you fall, that's all."

No one was home. I went into my room and turned on Carson's radio. *I've come to talk with you again,* a man sang out like he was tired, like he didn't really want to talk. I let my shoulders sway, my arms move a little, even my feet stepped with the song. The man sang light and whispery, in a way that caught me right under the ribs. A shiver kept trying to work its way down. The more I nodded with the music, the more cool air crept along my skin. Sweet and quick against my tongue, each breath came faster. Another song played now, but I moved just the same.

The clothes burned against my skin. I took off my shirt. It smelled like fire. I went to a mirror and raised up my arms. The ant welts looked mad. I pulled off my boots and socks, then I let my pants fall to the floor. I kicked them away. I put my hand right against the smooth skin. Naked. Like I was going to take a shower, but I didn't want to get wet, I wanted to have more of the air cool against the bites on my skin. I peeked out my bedroom door, then inched my way into the hallway. The carpet skitched under my bare feet. Down the hallway, into the living room where we'd read, I stood with the air snaking between my legs. I sat in the chair I'd sat in, reading, the night before. I'd sat in that same chair so many times, I knew the exact ribs of the velvet, but never like this, never with the nap of it so close in. I lay out. I let my fingers follow the blue veins of my abdomen down, to the dimple at my navel, down between my legs, then again to the blue veins tracing the inside of my thighs. My skin did not know if it wanted a blanket or an ice cube: it would quiet down only when I touched it, my fingers drifting back and forth.

Someone on the radio from the bedroom was talking, a woman, maybe an ad, or an announcement, I couldn't hear, but her voice joined in the music that I still had, and together, her voice and the lost music carried right to the edge of my skin. The fabric touched me everywhere, until I was so stiff and full I was afraid to touch anything else. But I couldn't help it, I did, until a shudder, so quick and so hard that it took my breath, ran down my entire body.

The fullness went away in a most beautiful silence. I couldn't move. I didn't want to put on my clothes. The music stayed with me, and I let my head move with it, and I loved it, and I wished it would quit.

I'd never realized how close my own skin was to me. Just thinking about putting clothes against my skin right then started voices and clanging in my head, louder and louder.

I wandered outside through the long grass, to where I could hear nothing but the softest water falling. I followed the simple sound to the edge of the pool. The water, the clear-green, cold water of the pool! When I put my hand to it, the pain in that hand stopped.

I slid in. It was so perfect! I splashed, and laughed. I lay back, letting it wet the back of my hair. It touched where I'd hit my head, and I realized then that my head had been pounding the whole time. Only my face was hot now, only my face still burned, and I went under. Silence, perfect silence. I wanted to go deeper. I wanted to lie on the very bottom for hours. I wanted my dad to come home and call for me, to keep calling until he came outside, to reach in, and carry me inside. And I wished he could do it without having to safety pin my tongue to my cheek.

In Working Order

WHEN I TOOK MY FIRST BREATH, after the long quiet under
the water, I realized how much we had come to the wrong
place. We were always getting lost. Too many tangles and
wrong turns—the air just weighed too much.

My dad didn't say anything about the ant bites when he
came home, even though they covered my face and neck, and
he didn't get mad that I hadn't packed anything. That night he
called my mom. I couldn't hear through my fever what they
said. Even the few words he said straight to me came from so
far away that I had to keep looking at him or the words would
be lost. That night I slept hard. When I finally got up, I found
a suitcase at the foot of my bed that I didn't recognize. When
we walked out to the car, he held one hand under my elbow,
like he knew something was wrong with me. He still didn't
say anything about the ant bites. I didn't realize that we were
getting into a strange car until we'd closed the doors.

"What's this?" I asked.

He tapped the dashboard. "A Coupe deVille. Cadillac." I sank into the soft leather seats. It smelled like the inside of a work glove. The huge, shiny dashboard even had wood inlaid in it. And there was so much room, I could stretch my legs all the way out in front of me. "Got a deal on it," he said. He stretched his arms from one side of the seat to the other. "I figured, as long as we'll probably be gone, we'll be calling this home. And it's about time we lived somewhere decent."

"When are we coming back?" I said. "What about the job? Did you quit?"

He smiled with his teeth. "Well," he held up his bandaged left arm, "I guess you could say that we finished that job ahead of schedule. One thing about the construction business. It's no goddamn place for anyone who's not got everything in working order. And I think you could fairly say that as far as I'm concerned, right now, not everything's in working order."

So we drove. He talked like he did before we lost the house, when he used to carry me around to the jobsites and lumberyards and coffee shops, when he could wave his hand and lift up his voice and go on about life, just like it was a treasure he had discovered, when he'd explain to me about doing the right things, about giving drunks and cons and people who'd fallen a chance to work, about standing up in school for the fat kids or the dumb kids, about owning all kinds of new businesses, what he would name them and what kind of buildings he would build, about getting the finest education for me so that for the rest of my life I would never be held back by something I couldn't do. In the car across the Florida Panhandle and the Alabama Gulf Coast, for the first time in such a long long time, he said all those things again, and even though my skin burned and pricked, I listened and listened, his words floating warm through my chest. I had forgotten that we used to laugh around the dinner table about him running away from ghosts in the dark after his Boy Scout meetings, or that I used to see him kiss my mom until she would laugh too hard to kiss anymore and she would slap him sweetly on his shoulder. I had forgotten so much and now I saw that if I could just make the time we were talking like this last, if I could somehow bring him to my mom again the way he was driving across Florida and Alabama, then she would want him back again.

He told me that when we got to Northern California we'd see trees, huge trees. I told him that my favorite thing about Florida was the live oak trees, with their branches like cantilevers, and I told him that I found out that they lost most of their leaves in the spring, not the fall. He said that he thought the live oaks just got plain tired, they couldn't hold up their branches, and they gave up their leaves so they had the strength to make it through the summer without all the weight. It was not exactly the way I remembered it from what I'd heard, but it was better, because the way he explained it, the leaves and the trees were connected to life, to more magnificent things.

He planned, he said, to build the house again, only bigger and stronger. He would send me through Harvard, to medical school or law school or seminary, and he would give Carson even better. She would come home to thoroughbred horses and she would wear those dresses that girls in private schools wore, and have her hair done by a man.

To all of this, hour after hour, I listened. The road disappeared before us. I counted the white lines, I read every billboard, every word that I could before we passed it, then I tried to remember everything that it said. I thought of questions to ask him, about shaving and real estate and checking accounts, but I didn't ask him. A few times his old anger showed, his jaw grinding, his neck muscles swelled with blood. And his hand hurt all the way up his arm, sometimes so bad that his face turned white and he'd sweat. But I only had to look out the window, to lay my head against the humming glass, and I heard thousands of miles of road.

I did know, even then, that he was lying. I knew we really had nowhere to end, that driving too fast all the way to Seattle wouldn't make my mom change her mind about anything. But where else could I be?

So I stayed. I thought of different ways to ask him if I could drive, but I never did. I was too old to sit on his lap now, too old just to hold the steering wheel. I tried to listen as carefully as I could, but every day, the more closely I listened, the more I wondered if he was really talking to me at all.

We left Texas at four in the morning and drove straight to a town in Arizona called Fort Huachuca. They had hills in the distance, and no wind. Sand came at the edges of the streets, eating at the few grass lawns. The houses all had flags but the flags didn't fly. The people moved like they were sad. We walked around a while, not going anywhere especially. I didn't know why, and I didn't ask, I just went where my dad went. Our footsteps scratched in the sand on the pavement and concrete. Army trucks drove out from a twelve foot chain-link fence around a base, down the street that led out of the town to the flat desert. As far as I could tell, we were hours from anywhere, any other town, any place for the trucks to go.

"You feeling all right?" he asked. I was still blurry-eyed from long morning hours in the car. "Something wrong?"

"Does Mom know we're coming?" I tried to ask like I had just thought of it.

"You see that church?" he pointed across the street. "I'd like to build a church like that someday." The building did not seem to belong to the town, it was so tall and the white paint was so clean.

"It used to take hundreds of years to build a cathedral like the ones they have over in Europe," he said. "Men would work their entire lives, never see it done. I read," he folded his hands, "that they would bury some of the workers right into the walls and foundations." He stopped, thinking. "Do you ever think about dying?"

I had no idea why he asked the question. "Sometimes," I said. "Sometimes I think about that kind of stuff."

And he looked at me like I was really there with him.

"I've tried to listen, you know," he said. "I can't keep up with what you say, but I've tried to listen, anyway. I know I've made mistakes. But you're the world to me, my family is. You're the only thing that matters. I feel like, what with losing that house and all, things really changed on us. You ought to have friends. Like your mother says. You ought to go on back to church, and—"

"I don't really think that much about that stuff anymore, Dad."

He raised his hand like he wanted to touch me. "I know," he said. "I know that. I didn't mean to start in about church. I remember what Har Lee used to say about that. He was about the only person I knew in Laurinburg who gave a shit about me, and he was about the only one with the guts to say he didn't have any use for a church."

"Whatever happened to Har Lee?" I asked.

"Well, he went off to the Army. He wasn't gone four months, and the next thing I know, there he is, right where he always stood, right outside Riggin's Drug Store, leaning against a lamppost smoking a Chesterfield. But something was wrong, I could see it right off. His eyes wouldn't quit jumping. Not a week later, at two in the morning he plowed down Main Street at eighty miles an hour and wrapped his car around a tree. So he's dead. But you know what his mother said at his funeral? I'll never forget it. She was just standing next to the coffin, talking to a group of us kids, and she said, *This boy didn't much believe in God, and I never could get him through a church service. And I know there's people here today who probably thought the boy was nothing more than a flashy bum, maybe even a coward. And whatever good he done I don't guess would last. I reckon he might just be in hell. If that's the case, though, all I got to say is, it's about time God started listening to a prayer now and then. I prayed for that boy all my life, and I want you to look now, I might as well of been trying to move Buck Mountain into my back yard.*

"And some old man came up and took her right out of that funeral parlor like she was crazy for what she said. And that," my dad said, spreading his fingers, "about sums up what I think about the whole ball of wax as far as God goes. I'd just as soon tell it to Har Lee. Even if he's gone to hell, at least he could hear what someone was saying to him."

I wished I'd worn shorts—the sweat had already started dripping down my legs in the blue jeans.

"Not much of a town, here, is it?" He dropped a cigarette to the broken sidewalk. "I came through a place just like this when I went AWOL, right after I hopped that train. That goddamn thing didn't stop for hours, I thought it was going to go clear into Mexico. Then there we were in the middle of the night, in the middle of so goddamn much desert I thought the whole damn world had just packed up and left. So I took my chances and skipped off." A car drove by, so slowly that it looked like it might stop at any moment, but it went on. "Then they brought me out here—right here to this very Army base—after I turned myself in, right back out to the desert. Survival training, they called it. What a goddamn place."

I started thinking maybe we weren't going to Seattle after all, maybe we'd just come to see this town again. We might go other places too, to the Mission Inn where he'd met my mom, or even to the place where he'd killed that guy. Maybe that was it—we'd retrace all those steps, and at the end he'd come clean of it all. My dad walked full ahead of me, dwarfing the street. We passed a movie theater, no different from the ones I'd seen before, but now it struck me that I'd hardly ever seen a movie except in school—and I didn't know why. I'd been to a movie once, with my mom, but I couldn't remember what it was. There were so many places like that to go, to see—baseball games, Chinese restaurants, fun places, places I'd heard other kids talking about, and all at once a longing for these things hurt in my chest. What if, once, we could really go places where other people went?

When we left, I wondered how it was that a place like Fort Huachuca had managed to work its dust into my skin. It made me want to breathe the oven air, to stretch out on the smooth sand and bake until I came from the desert the way my dad had come from the desert after his court-martial, a man who had learned to survive.

For the first while he drove, I thought more about places we could go, especially cities, even New York, that we could look at the Empire State Building, or we could walk on the Brooklyn Bridge and I could tell him what I knew about it, about how John Roebling had died before it was built and how his son who took over got the bends from the pressure, from working in the caissons, as they were trying to dig down to bedrock—bedrock they never found—and almost died.

"It won't take fifteen minutes," my dad said, almost excitedly. "I want him to see you, that's all. You'll see what West Point means. Wait till he opens the door and sees me, and sees you."

I didn't know now what my dad was talking about. "Where are we going?" I asked him.

"I told you. I told you already. You don't hear me. I got directions in town. We're going to Jack Levi's house. He lives near here."

"You mean the Jack Levi I'm named after, the guy who helped you out?"

He nodded. We were at a wall, some kind of dirt wall, with an iron gate.

"Dad," I said, "why are we here? Why did we come to this place?"

"I told you," he said, "this is the guy who can write a letter, and just like that you're into West Point, or Harvard, or whatever. You name it. Christ, listen up. And pull it together here."

He laid a hand on the iron gate. "It's adobe," he said, pointing through the bars to the house. "Basically, it's a foot thick wall of mud. Stays very cool." The brownness of the adobe walls and the redness of the roof made the house look like it had grown from the desert on its own. But it didn't fit very well. A wild collection of crumbling wood and tin outbuildings lay off the back. Grass grew in the packed sand along the drive. I could see now, too, that some of the roof tiles were cracked, and some of the black tinted windows were broken. "It's an old mission, probably," he said. "It could have been a hospital, or a monastery, who knows what, but they used to build these places strong enough to keep out all kinds of roughnecks, bandits. Anybody else, too." He pointed to the ridge of broken glass on top of the adobe wall. "Armies used them too. That's what the Alamo was. A mission." He rang the buzzer but no one answered. "I'm telling you, it's going to be a surprise when he sees us. This is the one man, more than anyone else in the world, who I can say was there when I needed him. He saw through all the bullshit. Through all my bullshit, through the Army's, through everything. I'd been thinking about stopping in here all along. God, it's been years."

A man came to the gate, and I thought we'd come to the wrong place. From all I'd heard about Captain Jack Levi—his intelligence, his courage, his Congressional Medal of Honor— I'd never seen a picture. But I knew the man in front of us wasn't him—he was too small, almost my size. And this man's hair was long, wavy, and totally gray, not dark and bristling like a soldier's. He didn't say a word when he opened the door, he just looked me and my dad over, head to foot.

"Hi, Captain Levi," my dad said with a hushed voice.

"Everest," he said, so delicately I wondered if he wasn't sure of the name. He wore baggy white clothes that looked like pajamas, and his thin feet were bare. "It's you. And is this . . . is this Levi?"

I nodded.

"Well, I must invite you both in. I must make some coffee. As I remember, you are a great coffee drinker, Everest." He brought us in and left us standing beside each other.

Inside, a rich dust covered huge carved walnut tables and chairs. The air tasted good, like clean mud and cigars. Everywhere, things were broken: drawer pulls held by only one screw, cracks in the cabinet glass, splintered wood sculptures, even the walls had pocks. Boxes lined the walls, old boxes filled with more broken things, wires, gears, old radios, chunks of wood.

It was the paintings covering the walls, though, that I couldn't believe. They hung in giant, dusty frames and some of the canvases were torn. The colors didn't stay put but moved over one another. It made me want to touch them— even the ashy blue faces that were twisted around black lips and white eyes, like they were screaming. On the wooden floor, I saw splashes of color so intense they were about to burst into flames, like the paintings had been painted right where they hung.

The people in the paintings were all naked, bent women with wrinkled breasts, kids with pink thighs, a tall black woman raising up her babies to a cross, a church with people dancing in the windows. The bodies didn't look real; they were smeared with reds and greens, and they had rainbows dripping from strange wounds, or had nails going up an arm, or flames for hair. Parts of the canvases weren't painted at all, while other parts had been painted so hard that the edges had been worn almost through.

"It's like they're alive," I said to my dad. He was looking at one with his eyes closed. A narrow doorway led to another room, with another carved walnut table, this one big enough for twelve people to sit around. More paintings, more swarming colors and twined bodies.

"You're nodding. You like this?" Captain Levi asked in a watery voice, right beside me. He held out a cup of coffee with a dry brownie wrapped in a paper napkin. "These are all people who have really lived. The way they really lived." A pale woman looked out at me from one of the paintings, coming from a field, her arms black up to the elbows. Behind her, a boy about my age, also pale but black to the elbows, carried a heavy burlap sack over one shoulder. "This woman had eight kids by the time she was twenty-five, and her husband died when the flu epidemic hit. The boy behind her went into an orphanage after this harvest. They're getting in tobacco."

I wanted to ask him why they would work out in the field naked, but I didn't. "So," Captain Levi said to my dad, "you two look like you've been on a hard road." He pointed to my dad's bandaged arm.

"Thumb got cut off, Captain," my dad said. "And sewed back on."

Captain Levi turned to me. "Actually, it's lieutenant colonel. I retired a lieutenant colonel. But that's all behind me. I'm just Jack, now. And I have to admit, at first I thought you had some kind of acne. But now I'd say—fire ants?" It took me a moment to realize he was talking to me. I nodded. "I suspect," he said, "you've been running a fever after that kind of tangle."

My dad looked closely at me. I sat down in a chair so huge and soft and red that I had to lean forward to see out of it. "I think the last I heard from you," Jack Levi said, "this child was just born. And now?"

When my dad started talking I couldn't believe it was his voice, the words were so small and they didn't echo at all, like the paintings were eating them. What he said was mostly true—about Carson and how she loved animals, about the construction work he'd been doing, and the moving, about losing the house and my mom spending some time in Seattle. It all sounded so quiet and normal, the good things and bad things.

He lied, too, though, and about things I couldn't understand. He didn't say that we were on our way to bring my mom back or anything like that, he said that he had decided to stay in Seattle, that he already had a job there, waiting for him, and that he was thinking about buying a townhouse. He said that he'd been painting too, and doing woodcarvings, that for the past few months he'd been painting the faces of great men who had lost. "You ever read the story of Chief Joseph?" my dad asked him. "I read where when he said he wasn't going to fight anymore, he pointed to the sun and said that the sun would go down, but for him, it wouldn't come back up."

Jack Levi nodded. "So," he said to me, "are you an artist like your father?"

I liked the chime of his voice, and I wanted to tell him yes, that I painted too, that sometimes I thought about going to live in a desert too, to a place that was totally quiet, with no trees or grass, and seeing nothing but the sand and the sky. "I used to draw some," I said, "I might do it again sometime."

He laughed, kindly. "I remember something your dad painted once," he said. "It was a little confusing, but it had good lines."

"I never really learned how to draw things the right way," I said. I wanted to tell him about the smudges, the torn paper, the hands that were never right, the face that never really told a story, that it was only wood that I could draw, that I knew so many different grains.

He pulled a cigar out of his pajama shirt pocket, "I guess you could say I prefer crucifixions. But of ordinary people." He lit the cigar grandly. "At any rate. Everest. Tell me about your wife."

My dad reached for a pack of cigarettes from his shirt pocket, but he didn't get one. "She's—" he moved his hands like he would have the right word, then let them rest awkwardly on his knees. He looked, and I looked, to corners of the dusty room. The walls were too thick, too high. The back of the red leather chair he sat in rose over his head. When, I wondered, did the gray get into his hair? His eyes, ever since the hospital, had too much water in them. "The thing about Nora," he said, his voice thinning, "she's the mother of my children. I don't care if she writes her articles—she's writing little things for the paper up there—that's fine. I don't care if she wants to go to ball games with her sister, or go to movies. She knows I don't like to have a lot of people around. I can't listen to the talk. I can't stand the chitchat. I just want to be left alone. But I've got a family. These kids—" he nodded to me without looking, "he's got a future. And Nora, she's got to be there. I've put too much into this family, into building some-thing, into educating them—" His face was red. "Goddamn this hand hurts," he said, trying to cradle it to him.

"You might want some aspirin," Jack Levi said without moving. "So. I take it she's an attractive woman."

"Yes," I said, before I knew it.

"Yes," said Jack Levi, his eyes searching my face. "Yes, I might have guessed as much. Fair-skinned, fair-haired."

"And," he said to my dad, just as softly, "it sounds like you might be considering, shall we say, holding on to what you've got?"

My dad moved uneasily in the red chair. "I'm considering a lot of things," he said.

"Oh, I know that feeling, I know that feeling," Jack Levi said, rubbing his thin hands together. "I saw it immediately when I opened the door. I suppose," he said to me, "your father has told you about the circumstances under which we met?"

I nodded.

"He knows," my dad said, his eyes small, "I'm no saint."

Jack Levi laughed. He perched at the edge of his chair and

reached for a lighter, and lit the cigar he'd been holding. "I am not an old man, yet," he said, pushing back his gray hair, speaking each letter of each word so carefully, so slowly, that it made a kind of music. He kept moving his thin hands in little lines. The kindness in his eyes was sharp, blue. He smiled like a father to me. "But I'm old enough. I abhor violence, all violence. I don't want to hear anymore about wars, people who burn children." He turned to the painting behind him, of a delicate, cocoa-skinned woman whose back was lashed and bleeding. "Seems like people have to have the shit beat out of them before other people pay attention."

A peculiar silence settled around us when he finished. "Anyway," he said, "enough. You've come for a reason. You need my help."

The whole time Jack Levi was talking, my dad had his face turned away from us, never moving. "I've got to protect my family," he said.

They were talking in such low, dead tones, saying things I couldn't keep together, my body sank into the chair. The more they talked the harder it was to move, as though the rumble of their words was sticking in my bones.

Jack Levi stood, his pajama top flowing as he raised his arms. "On the other hand, you could call it sacrifice. What could be worse than taking a life? I've heard of children who have lost a parent say 'if I could only have one more hour.' Even grown men talk like this. Imagine you caused pain like that," he said, not looking at my dad but at me. "But then someone says 'it's okay.' Someone else takes the blame, for you. You go on with your life, you don't have to do anything, just go and be free!"

I could not believe my dad was sitting so still. He didn't even clench his fists.

Jack Levi nodded now. "But that's not the same as being forgiven. There's no such thing as that, because you always know. You did it. That moment," he said, holding his thumb and forefinger a fraction of an inch apart, "is yours, and it's yours for the rest of your life."

Why didn't my dad say anything? Why was Jack Levi talking about these things like he was holding my dad in a glass jar, like he was studying him?

My dad stood up. "We're just out seeing the country, really. I figured Levi here was about old enough to appreciate some natural beauty. The Grand Canyon, all that."

"Well, if you're out seeing things, I know something you might find valuable. I've got a collection. Nothing like a museum, I'll grant, but still, it's probably more worthwhile than sitting in a dark study listening to an old man. Hell," he said, nodding to me, "I was getting fidgety myself." He walked away. At first we weren't sure if we should follow him or wait, but after a while when he didn't come back, we went after him.

The house was a maze, endless doorways, and I know we passed two kitchens before we came to the room. Glass cabinets lined every wall, and in the cabinets were more kinds of guns than I ever knew existed. At first he showed us guns that looked like they came from movies—Smith and Wessons, Colts, Saturday night specials, rifles with beautiful wooden stocks, even a Derringer that had a place where he said it had been nicked by a bullet. The barrels smelled of steel and gunpowder in a way that rang in my teeth. He aimed some of them at the window, cocking them, and letting the hammers click. He handed my dad some of them, telling us little things about where he'd bought them, how old they were, and what they were good for.

Some of the guns didn't look so familiar, though. He had

pistols that looked like they could shoot lasers, they were so sleek and polished. He pulled out the longest, widest drawer I'd ever seen, from below one of the glass cabinets, where I didn't even know there was a drawer. "You'll appreciate this," he said to my dad, and he picked up a smooth, black pistol with a barrel as long as my forearm.

He reached back further in the drawer and pulled out a box of cartridges. "Give it a go?" he asked my dad. "And one for you, Master Levi," he said, taking a pistol from a desk in the middle of the room, "Smith and Wesson .38. Careful with this one—I keep it loaded. So, it's not pointed except where you want a bullet to go. Safety's on, but still."

I'd never held a gun before, so I didn't know what to expect. The first thing I noticed was how heavy it was, an important, reassuring heaviness. Even so, it wasn't uncomfortable at all—in fact, it was shaped perfectly for my hand. The rubber grips were slightly warmer than the metal. He had a tooled leather holster hanging on the wall, and for a moment I thought I might ask if I could wear it, but I caught myself. He picked up a long roll of paper and we walked out through the kitchen to a kind of long courtyard. We went out a gate at the end of it to an empty desert. Jack Levi was still barefoot, still in his pajamas. He brought out a table and poured out some bullets. I couldn't figure out what we could shoot at until he walked into the desert. He picked up a pole and slid it right into the ground. It had some kind of board on top, like a sign, but with nothing on it. He unrolled the paper targets he'd brought with him and clipped one to the signboard.

The house was behind us. With the sun so clean on my face, I thought how easy it would be to live in a place like this. I always thought I loved trees, loved climbing them, but now I realized that I wanted away from trees. And bushes, even grass. I wanted ground around me that was just as empty and simple as this was. I wanted nothing, and lots of it.

My dad held the pistol up with his good hand. He fired. The sound, as loud as it was, did not startle me. In fact, the instantaneous click and bang, with no echo, seemed to cut though a kind of fog in my mind. Nothing nagged about the sound, it simply came and went, cleanly, leaving only a single, soft ringing in my ears that faded smoothly. I wanted to hear it again. The bullet kicked up a tiny cloud from the target.

Jack Levi put a tiny kind of telescope to his eye. "About two and a half low," he said. "Your dad," he said to me, "could shoot so clean. Like he could stop the wind."

My dad fired again. "About a half high," Jack Levi said. The next shot hit the small black center, I could see from where I stood. Shot after shot, the slow perfect sounds didn't run together, but went off like hammers hitting nails square on the head.

After eight shots we walked out to the target together. The first two shots were easy to see—exactly above and below the bull's-eye. The next ones had simply torn out a hole about an inch wide from the center of the target.

"You know," Jack Levi said to me as we walked back, "you might want to start with bottles. Just a minute." He went back into the courtyard and came out with a milk crate full of bottles, then walked out and set them up on the crate. "Now," he put his hand over mine and lifted the revolver, "you hold it out like so, line up the sights, take a breath, and blow it out real nice and easy. You never pull the trigger. You squeeze it, firm, like you're pulling right through it. When you get good, you can even pull the trigger between heartbeats. That is, of course, a matter of listening to a very quiet thing." He let go of my hand.

I raised the pistol, the smoothness of his palm still

lingering on my knuckles. I took in the breath like he said, and let the air seep out again, steady. I listened for what seemed like a long time, but I could not hear my heart beating. I listened so long I had to take another breath, and then I shot. I missed. The recoil surprised me, throwing my hand up so high I was afraid I'd let go of the pistol. Sand kicked up to the right of the bottles. The next time I aimed more carefully, making sure that the sights lined up exactly, that each edge matched. I missed again, and again. The sound of my pistol hung in the air longer than when my dad had shot, and was more metallic, even screeching a bit, but I wanted to hear it again. I liked the recoil too, it was like I was touching the bullets as they went off.

"They're going right," Jack Levi said. "You're pulling the trigger with your arm instead of your finger. Always happens." This time I tried to relax my arm muscles. I still missed, but it was closer.

"Look here now," he came close again and clamped his fingers to the top of my head. "You're not keeping your head still. You've got some kind of—some...well," he said, letting go of my head, "you're fine. Just take your time, and breathe. That's the whole thing really, the breathing."

I took as easy a breath as I ever had, and pulled the trigger. The bottle shattered with a quick, light music of its own. I hit more, and we shot for about an hour. My arm ached from the careful holding of the pistol.

"Let me show you one thing," Jack Levi winked at me, "let you see why they make different caliber guns." He went to the courtyard and came back out with two plastic milk jugs filled with water. He set them out where we'd set the bottles. "Now," he said, "take the .38 and drill one of those jugs." I did, first shot. A stream of water trickled to the ground. "Now," he said, "take this." He handed me the big pistol my dad had been using. "It's a .44." I raised the gun just like I'd done the smaller one, aimed, and squeezed. The sound hit me with such force that I thought the gun had backfired in my face. I couldn't find my breath at first. By the time I remembered where I was, they were laughing, kindly. When I finally took a breath, I knew from how cold my face had become that I was pale. Then I laughed too, shaking my head.

"Gives you a licking no matter which end of the gun you're at," Jack Levi said. He took the gun from my limp arm. "Though I'd have to say, the business end is, quite surely, a bigger mess." He fired, and the milk jug exploded. It was gone.

"Whoa," I whispered. "How'd it do that?"

"Pressure," he said. "The bullet hits the water, so hard and so fast and so big, and that water gets so hot and pushed around, it's got nowhere to go. So it goes everywhere at once. End of story."

We walked back inside and left the guns on the desk, the barrels still warm, and went to the room with the paintings.

"Gentlemen," Jack Levi said, "it's been a real goddamned pleasure to spend the time with you."

I was used to leaving places, of course, by then. I had a way of looking at a house for the last time, starting inside, room by room, then standing in front and counting the windows, taking in the way the siding ran or the color of the brick, the trees, the curve of the driveway, then closing my eyes and seeing it all over again. I wanted to do that when we left Jack Levi's house. I wanted to make sure I never forgot the exact shade of his mud walls, or the way the desert stretched out so silently from the back of the house, or even the paintings that were making my eyes swim before we left. We left so quickly, though, with so much dust kicking up from the car, I couldn't see any of it. I couldn't remember any of the words Jack Levi used either. But he'd been good to me. His voice came kindly to my ear, he knew who my dad was and he wasn't afraid of it, he let me hold a gun for the first time, and I liked him.

Duval really surprised me this morning. *We're at Crowders Mountain, in the North Carolina foothills. It took two hours to drive here, and I can't believe he's actually going to pay me to climb even though we're not working.*

I try to thank him, but he won't hear it. "You're all right," he tells me, "all you need is some experience."

I've never actually climbed on rock before. We use ropes and harnesses on the steeples, so I know how that goes, but this is different. There's parts where the cliff actually angles out over my head, so I'm kind of upside down. Duval's on belay, and he calls out where to put my hands and feet.

I fall, and I'm hanging off.

He's letting me down so I can make another go of it. "It's weird," I say. "They say freezing to death is the way to go. I mean, like opposed to burning."

"Falling," he says. "The landing kills you, the old joke, you know, but really, if I had to go, I'd want the ride. I just hope I'd have the sense to know it, that instead of trying to grab something that wasn't there, I'd be in the moment, totally." *He checks my ropes.* "But don't get me wrong," *he laughed,* "I'd just as soon never find out."

I think about telling him what my dad used to say about falling up, but the kind of thing we're doing now, even on the steeples, it doesn't really work.

A Map

WHEN WE LEFT THE CLAY HOUSE, the night had settled into the clouds. It was beautiful, but the darkness was spooky and we seemed to be driving away from anywhere we might stop.

My dad pulled over to the side of the road. "I was thinking," he said, "you might want some practice at the wheel." He smiled. "What do you say?"

I couldn't believe it. I couldn't even answer him, for fear that whatever I'd say might make him change his mind. He stepped out and I slid over.

"Go ahead and raise the seat up," he said. "It's electric." I did, until I could see the hood, right over top of the steering wheel. He showed me how to start it. I knew it already, but I didn't say. "First off," he said, "you got to know where the brake's at. Hold your foot there for a second till you're comfortable, till you know where it's at. Now, shift to drive, and when you let the brake off, you don't need to hit the gas—just let the engine get you going for right now. Right."

I was barely moving, holding my foot right over the brake. I tapped the gas. We'd gone only a few feet, and he pointed me off the road to a path into the desert.

"Don't look right down the hood," he said, "keep your eyes up, down the road a ways. You'll actually drive straighter. And the stuff that's close up, you'll see anyway."

I gradually went faster, up to twenty-five miles an hour. The dirt track we were following was mostly straight, but with enough curves to make it interesting. I didn't look around where we were, I just remember it stretching out from us in every direction. We didn't go anywhere—we didn't wind up at some hidden canyon, or an oasis, or a town, we just kept going for the longest time, probably a half-hour or so, until we wound up in a place where all we could see was hard sand, all one color but about a hundred shades of that color.

The whole time, all I heard, and saw, and felt was the driving—the car and the road. My dad didn't talk, I didn't think, we just made our way. When we stopped to turn around and head back, my hands ached from gripping the wheel.

I wanted nothing more right then than to be sixteen, to have a license, and to be able to drive, anywhere I wanted.

My dad drove when we started on the road again. When we settled into a stretch of highway he cleared his throat. "You're not saying anything."

"I was wondering where else we were going." I knew we were going to Seattle, but I hoped maybe he had somewhere else in mind too, another place for us to see. The speedometer needle crept upwards.

"I'm going to be forty years old in no time," he said. "Look at all this," he waved his hand across the landscape. "When I was a kid I never imagined a real place like this existed—I only thought these places were in movies, you know? I think sometimes about just turning off, going down some road and keeping going, then just getting out and walking, until I'm so far away I can't find my own way back."

"Can you tell me where we're going?" The needle hovered between ninety and a hundred miles an hour, ticking like a turn signal. It thrilled me a little, but then tiny raindrops pelted the windshield and disappeared in the wind. Now I was sure we were going too fast. The car glided smooth as glass. I wasn't sure he knew how fast he was going.

"You don't always wind up where you think you will. That's something I think I've learned recently, from recent events. Like on a job, where things never work out the way the blueprints say they will."

He started saying everything at once then, like he wanted to go everywhere at the same time. He was sorry about all of it. All he wanted was to be a *good man*. We were going a hundred. The speed locked in my knees. I tried to think if I'd said anything to make him drive the way he was driving. "I wanted a family, halfway decent kids, money, and educations—" he brought his hand down on the steering with each word now, and the car inched to the side each time. "To be able to read a goddamn restaurant menu. To do the *right thing*. But every time, it's the same thing, they're all waiting to kick me back where I started." His eyes moved deliberately, like he had to remind himself to blink.

I didn't want to hear him talk anymore. Even if his voice came from the radio speakers, low and kind, it had ground out, gone sandy. And now, I had no idea whether he was going to drive us off the road into a concrete bridge abutment or turn around and just go home.

"What the hell happened? Have you talked to her?" He rocked in his seat. Then he talked about everything he'd already talked about before, the same lies, the same promises, but now it was different. Now he spit them out like they were burning his mouth. And we were driving straight to the end of the lies at a hundred and five miles an hour, and we wouldn't stop, I knew, until someone got hurt.

"I don't know what to say to you. My whole family is gone." He looked wildly from the road to the tree—to me. "Jesus Christ," he said incredulously, "What's the matter?" He jammed his cigarette out the window.

"I got to go," I said, talking between my heartbeats. "I got to go to the bathroom. Bad."

"Do you need me to pull over?" I hardly recognized his voice; in the blink of an eye it was warm with worry, almost soothing. "Don't make yourself sick," he said. "Here, we'll get off right here." As soft as an airplane, the car floated down the off-ramp. We pulled into a restaurant, the Painted House, and I realized how relieved I was to see people around. "Listen," he said as he stopped the car. "Sorry. My hand, it hurts so bad I can hardly hold my head together. Let's get something to eat. Okay?" he said. "I know it's been hell for you too. Let's just start over, all right? I need you."

He walked from the car without waiting for me. I was glad he'd left. I'd come to a single point when we stopped, I just wanted one thing, to know where we were. If I knew that, I'd know if we were still headed for Seattle. I wanted a map. I checked the glove box, but nothing. I fished my hand under my seat, then under his.

I knew it was a gun without looking. I didn't move it. My

hand, when I pulled it out, was white, like the pistol had frozen it.

What was so strange was that it was like I'd known it was there all along, but now, now that I'd actually touched it, I wanted to hold it, to carry it with me. I shut the car door. I stopped one last time in the parking lot to look at the car, to make sure it was still there, and that's when I saw that the license tags were from New Jersey. I stepped closer to make sure. I said the words *New Jersey* a few times. I thought, well, but nothing made sense. He had to have changed the plates, pulled them off some car at a rest stop or something without my noticing it.

I couldn't add it up—the gun, the plates, the fast driving— except to know that things were bad. I didn't know if someone was after us because he'd kicked somebody in the mouth in Michigan just before we left, or if he'd been stealing money in Florida, or if we were heading into trouble, not away from it.

The restaurant clatter was deafening. I passed the cash register at the door, and stopped in the middle of the restaurant, trying not to let my eyes show what I'd seen. I spotted the signs for the bathrooms, and walked over as straight as I could. Just as I turned the corner, something stabbed my right shoulder. I had run into a coat hook. I swung around, so suddenly I was leaning over a table.

"Excuse me," I said, getting my balance against the edge of the table. The woman at the table pulled her kid to her. "I'm sorry," I said, backing toward the restrooms.

My hand, wet with sweat, slipped on the bathroom doorknob. When I opened the door, I caught myself in the mirror, and drew back at the sight of my face. My hair stood out in all directions, wet, and pushed into rows by my fingers. Then I laughed. I laughed at the way my face was translucent white. Even the ant bites had gone white, against the pink flowers of the wallpaper. There was not any color to my lips. I pinched my crotch, making myself wait until the pink flowers stopped vibrating. The room was spacious; there was a soft chair where I could sit if I had to, except that now I really could barely hold it another minute. I tried to find the urinal.

Someone screamed, just for a split second and I wondered, did I miss the gunshot? Had I heard it, or was he killing someone with just his bare hands? I turned. The woman, whose table I'd knocked into, stood in the open doorway with her kid. On the door, over her moppy red hair, I saw the Ladies' sign. The door shut. I turned again to the mirror, and laughed at myself. I could hear the noise from the restaurant, of people talking and dishes and even the rain falling down the windows.

I sat down at the table with my dad, my hair combed, my face still cool from washing it. We ate quietly, and eventually the noise of the restaurant faded. I'd been hungry.

"Are you okay?" he asked when we got back to the car. "You haven't been getting into drugs or something, have you? Can you hear me?"

I had heard leaves, too. I knew it, but we were still in the desert. And no matter how hard I looked, I couldn't find a single tree.

Always Order What You Want

I KNEW THEN WHAT WE WERE HEADING FOR, and for the rest of the trip a single hum locked in all my muscles. He said something, some words here and there, but they didn't stick. I had one thought—if the voice that had followed me through the woods should break through the hum, I would do anything to stop it. I saw a bullet going through my head like it had that milk jug, and I could hear the sound of that moment so pleasantly in my bones.

I thought of how to call my mom, to warn her. It seemed like it would be such a simple thing, to walk over to a phone and dial the number, but I was never out of his sight. I had tried to come up with a good lie, but I knew that even if I had one, I wouldn't be able to tell it right. Every time we stopped, for gas or food, or to spend the night at the rest stop, sleeping in the car, I considered if I should run away. I knew I could do it—that I could get out before he could catch me—but I knew if I ran, by the time I called my mom and the police, he'd be in another car and they wouldn't know how find to him. And where would I go? I didn't even have a dollar—he kept all the money rolled up in his front pocket. I might take the gun, but what for? To shoot him? It was so real now that I knew exactly what would happen then, how he'd just walk right up to the barrel and take it out of my hands. No, if I took the gun I'd have to be ready, right at that moment, to shoot him.

He was going to do what he said he was going to do, which was to get my mom. And the more I thought about it, the more I figured that the best thing for me to do would be to stay with him, to try to keep him calm, to call if I got the chance, to stand in front of her when we got there.

I thought constantly, but every thought had to be pushed through, like trying to put a thread through a needle. I had to think to breathe, to swallow, to blink. And he was never more than a few feet from me, ticking through his own minutes, driving.

We checked into a Motel 6 in Seattle and headed straight to Frankie's. When we pulled in the driveway, Frankie came to the door, clutching her bathrobe around her. Her skin was smooth and pinkish, and the collar of the bathrobe was opened enough to show where her breasts started curving away. Her hair was longer and redder than I remembered. When I got out of the car she ran up to me like I'd just been pulled up from a well. She put her arms around me so tight that it was the only thing I could think about.

"Frankie," I whispered, my face still at her shoulder, "where's Mom? Be careful, he's..."

By then my dad was there. She shook his hand, still holding me to her.

"Where's Nora," he said right off. I looked at his hands; they were empty.

"You two must be exhausted," she said, clicking her tongue. "You look like you walked the whole way here. How long did it take? And Everest! What in the world did you do to your arm?"

"Five days," my dad moved his hand awkwardly through his hair. "We're fine. Fine. Nice to see you, Frankie. Where's Nora?"

Frankie did not seem to have a care in the world. She rubbed her bare foot in the grass. "I have to tell you, Ev, the sheriff's office down where you lived in Florida called. I wished you'd have called me. That company you worked for has been trying to find you. They say, well," she looked at me, a little sad. "Maybe we should go inside, or maybe, Levi, do you want to wait inside while I talk to your dad a minute? It's probably not too good to drag you into all this, now anyway."

The strain in my dad's voice was noticeable even though he was talking softly. "Frankie, I'm just asking where Nora—"

"She's not here right now." Frankie was not talking softly now. Then she turned again to me. I didn't know whether to stay or go. I didn't want to leave her outside with him unless I'd told her about the gun. "Levi, you know what? There's a Mariners' game tonight. Do you know that I'm an absolute nut about baseball?"

"Frankie, I'm not going to play around here." He was fighting to keep the anger from rising in his eyes. "I'm through with playing around. I want to get my family, what's left of it. We're building a house and I need my kids. I want Nora back here by tonight."

"I won't play around with you, Everest." She turned her hand in my direction. "Look at that boy, that precious boy."

More Like Not Running Away

He did not look. "When's the last time he slept? He looks like he doesn't know whether to stand up or fall down." She laid her hand on mine. "If you want what's best for everyone, turn around and take your Cadillac and your beautiful lies out of here. You left a mess in Florida. All I need to do right now is make one phone call—"

Seeing his face, it hit me that it might be Frankie he wanted to kill, not my mom, that maybe he thought it was Frankie who was taking everyone away from him. These thoughts were tiny slivers that I did not know how to sort.

"Frankie," I said suddenly. "Things are better. A lot better. I want to go with my dad. There's nothing to worry about, really. I just want to see my mom. That's all. I just really miss her. Can you just tell her that, and that we're staying—"

"Just tell her we'll be back tonight. No more games," my dad said. He started to say something else to Frankie, but backed away and opened his car door instead. He pushed his hands through his hair and started the car. Frankie let go of my hand. "Honey," she said quietly, "please just help him see, if you could just see your sister, how happy she is, with her friends here."

"He's got a gun," I said.

Me and my dad drove away, and all the way to the motel a fragile silence held us together.

He stood shaving in the motel mirror. I sat on the bed, thinking about what he would say when we ate, and trying to watch him shave. I asked him how much a brush and shaving mug would cost. We had still hardly spoken, and he was acting like he regretted not standing his ground at Frankie's.

He wiped his lips and picked up a cigarette. "Jesus Christ, I don't know," he said. The only light on in the room was the one over the mirror. He turned around, his eyebrows close together, and flicked an ash on the floor. "Are you still in your underwear? Get dressed, for Christ's sake. They'll take forever in the goddamn restaurant. And they wonder why nobody stays at Motel 6's anymore."

He pulled hard at the razor, and the blood mixed with with the soap on his chin. "Goddamn it," he said. I grabbed my pants from off the television. They were the pants my mom had bought just a day before we left Michigan, the pants I wore almost every day. They were ragged now at the cuffs, and they had grown soft and faded. When I'd tried them on in the store my mom had told me that I walked like a movie star. He splashed Old Spice on the cut, wiped his neck with a towel, and set his cigarette on the television. The cigarette and shaving lotion made him smell cleaner and younger. He put a starched shirt on over his still-wet shoulders.

"Is that the only thing you've got to wear?" he asked. "No wonder your aunt thinks you're falling apart."

I didn't answer. I pulled on my shirt that matched. It had frayed too. He paced around the room. "Let's go," he said, grabbing the key and his cigarette from the television.

"Just a minute." I tied one of my shoes and started looking for the other under the bed. "I can't find my other shoe."

He sat on the bed and lit another cigarette. "Goddamn it," he said, very softly like he meant it for himself. I looked under both beds. A guy on the television was trying to pick up a girl. Her kid was jabbering. She touched the guy on the arm. "Oh goddamn," my dad muttered again, grinding out his cigarette and jabbing the off switch on the television. I checked the bathroom.

The shoe was soaking wet, between the toilet and shower. A bug was squashed on the floor underneath it. I drew back, furious, wanting to throw it against the wall or the mirror, to go stand right in front of him, to tell him what a goddamn stupid thing it was to use my shoe and then just leave it there while he was in the shower. It was the only pair I had. I pulled it on, and the water drenched my sock.

"I'm ready," I said, hard. But he was gone. I opened the door a crack, and stuck my head out looking for him. The weather outside had turned almost cold. He was going down the walkway. A wind had picked up, and he walked even taller when he turned into it. He opened the door to the restaurant like it didn't deserve to stay on its hinges.

I started after him, but then I saw his car keys still on top of the TV. When I reached for them, I almost pulled my hand back. They made so much noise. I stuck them in my pocket, sneaked down the stairs, across the parking lot, opened the car door, reached under the seat, and pulled out the gun. It was heavy, and it smelled burned. I hadn't thought about what I'd do with it, and crouching in the car now I realized I couldn't just walk across the parking lot. I put the barrel in the waist of my pants and let my shirt hang outside.

I cut out of the car and walked as quick as I could back up the steps and into the room. I put his keys on the TV and left the room again, thinking now I might stash the gun behind the ice machine, a few doors up. The barrel sights kept sticking me in the groin, and it was harder and harder to walk right. Just as I got to the ice machine, I saw him, right there. I almost screamed.

"Where in the hell have you been?" He nodded to the restaurant. "Let's order the damn food. I'm hungry. I've got shit to do. Enough screwing around." He turned and I followed, struggling to walk as normally as I could.

He looked me over again when we got to the door, and I was scared he'd say something about my shirttail hanging out but he didn't. He dropped his cigarette to the rubber mat inside the door, and I stepped on it, kicked it under a table. No one was in the restaurant, and the chairs were up on about half the tables. There were huge brown stains on the ceiling from leaks, and everything smelled like fried seafood. The waitress handed us a menu without saying anything. When I sat down, the sight on the gun barrel cut hard into me, so hard I wondered if I was bleeding. She stood waiting for our order.

"Coffee," my dad said, "black." He brushed some salt from the table.

I couldn't think of anything I wanted. I ordered a BLT. He opened his menu. "Why don't you have a steak," he said. "You need to eat. A sandwich isn't going to fill you up. You've got steak, don't you?" The waitress nodded. Her skin was the color of fluorescent light. I nodded to her. She didn't ask how I wanted it.

He pulled the ashtray to him and lit a cigarette, blowing the smoke after the waitress. "Now," he said, rubbing his temples. "Tell me. What does Frankie want? Does she think I'm going to walk away and leave my family with a goddamn divorcee? You acted like you knew how to handle this, so tell me." I didn't look at him; I let my hand drift down to rest on my shirt, over the gun. To hide it better, but to know it was there, too. He went on. "I'm sick and goddamn tired of getting the rug pulled out from under me every time I try to stand up and give something to my children. I thought I could trust your mother to hold things together, but she's acting like it's over. It hasn't even started. For all I know, she's out right now whoring around this town. I get out of the goddamn hospital and you look like death. I can't even tell if you're able to think straight, and somehow it all seems like it's my fault. Your sister—"

The waitress brought the coffee. He lifted the cup to his lips, and spit it out. "It's cold," he said. His eyes flashed. The waitress took the cup back.

"So," he said, fanning out his hands. "That's where it is. It's up to you."

I couldn't stand the gun sight digging in me anymore. I'd been shifting back and forth in my seat, but when he said whoring around, I went ahead and reached under my shirt and adjusted the gun. I stood up now. I pulled the wet shoe from my foot, held it up, and squeezed it until the water dripped to the floor.

"You know," I said, my voice hot, "I don't give a damn who it's up to anymore. You're talking about my mother. And my sister. And I just wish you'd shut the hell up." The anger in his face washed right over me. "You don't even know how old I am. You don't know anything about my school. You tell me all about who you killed and what you're going to build and where you want me to go to college. But you never say anything about me."

I held my shoulders back. "And you got my goddamn shoe all wet." I hadn't been actually thinking about the gun— but once I'd started talking, I just knew that at some point he'd probably stand up, to come at me, and I was going to pull it out, aim it at him, and keep talking. The waitress had stopped in the middle of the restaurant.

The hardness left his face. His mouth would not stay still, even though his jaw muscles were locked. Sad waves came across his eyes, turning the corners red and making the dark parts glisten. There was nothing in him left that looked able to so much as lift a fist. "Okay," he said. "I'm finished."

He left. The silence in the restaurant was all his, it smothered everyone and everything. Tree branches snapped in the wind outside the window, but I was the only one who could hear them. My throat would not move.

I don't know how long I stood there. Eventually the waitress took a step, going about her business more slowly, like she'd seen this so many times before and she knew just to go on. I walked to the back of the motel. A chain-link fence eight feet high, rusted and pulled loose, stretched across the parking lot. I put my head against it. The wind ran over and over me until I felt nothing at all. I listened. Nothing. The wind, I thought, watching the tree branches beating back and forth in the dark, why not the wind? Why didn't the chain link rattle when I shook it? Cars went by, but no engines raced, no tires turned, no road hummed out. I took out the gun and laid the cool barrel to my cheek. Yes, I thought, yes. All I had to say to him was *This is as far as I can go.* I would not get in the car with him again.

I didn't know how to get to Frankie's house. I could see if she was in the phone book, or I could just go somewhere else, a park, or a restaurant, anywhere. I could wait. Until I found my mom. And I would tell her everything, about the gun, about him. She would never go back.

I thought I might need the gun later, so I put it in my pants again. I didn't want to go back to the room, but I needed money if I was going to get to my mom's. I would go up; if I saw him, or heard him, I'd just leave. But the door to our room was left open. The only light on was the one over the mirror. Two hundred dollars lay on the dresser. When I picked it up, I saw a carved block of wood, black walnut, waist-high, beside the bed. He must have had it in the trunk of the car. It took me a minute before I recognized it. Every feature of the face was smooth, but the creases, around the eyes and the mouth, were rough. I knew without any doubt that he had carved it himself, the wrinkles were so deep. And the eyes. So colorless, so empty, they cut trances in me. It had to be an Indian; probably Chief Joseph. My dad didn't really know much about Indians, except that they lost everything. And he admired that.

He'd taken an axe to it, and splintered the face and head. Glue showed in the seams. I knew what it was, a gift. For my mom.

A trunk lid slammed. He was in the parking lot, crouched on the pavement, shoving his arm all over under the seat. He saw me. And he knew I had it. He got in the car and started it full throttle. I ran out, the noise of the wind and the car and street and even the buzz of a streetlight all pounding in a rhythm that filled my chest. He didn't need a gun: he would go after her, if I didn't stop him. I tried to call out, but too many things were happening. I thought of pulling out the gun, but thought not yet, not yet.

His headlights were aimed at my eyes. I stretched my hand out to signal him to stop. As I ran toward him, his wheels spun against the pavement with a long, dry moan. I thought he didn't see me, so I stepped in his path, looking for him through the dark windshield, but I couldn't find his eyes. He wasn't slowing down, he wasn't turning away, the car was going so fast I could not even catch a breath to call out. The headlights stunned me. I raised my arms higher. He didn't slow, or turn. It was too late to reach for the gun now. I dove to the pavement just in time, his wheels only inches from my elbow. It took so long for the car to get past me, I saw so much of it—the smooth light off the hubcaps, all the dark, tangled parts underneath, the slow arc it made going past—I thought he'd stopped.

I lay there, in that moment, but the moment stuck. I considered that he might turn back around, but I didn't move. The blood came from scrapes at my forehead and hands, and I wondered if I'd actually been hit. I moved my arm. By the time I could roll over, my muscles started seizing. My stomach tightened until my face was pushed to my knees.

My head moved first, the old nodding but not easy, not quiet, this was like steel cables that had been holding it still were snapping. When my head brushed the pavement I began hearing it all at once, gunfire, screams, a high-speed car crash, over and over my dad's voice calling out a thousand words that would not string together, my mom's breath, and the wind, the wind that was trying to pull the motel building apart, trying to rip the branches from the trees, trying to find a way inside my head. By the time I could walk, the noises were so loud that I couldn't see more than a few feet in front of me.

I may have thought of calling Frankie, or the police, but it would have been impossible, impossible even to find the room, because I could see less and less with each step. A machine of noise was driving me. I could no more change where I was going than I could have called the birds down from the trees.

I climbed the chain-link fence to the motel pool. I put my shoes in; the water seeped in, stunning cold. But with each step I took into the water, the less I thought about, and the noises that had been wearing me down the last months sounded farther and farther away. My clothes got so heavy that I could hardly stand up. Quiet, quiet. When I got to my neck I did stop, I thought about my mom, that I needed to tell her something, but that thought drifted off. The bottom of the pool got suddenly steep and I slipped. My head went under, and I went down.

He was gone. And for the first time in a long time, I didn't have to go with him. The icy water pushed on my eardrums, the pressure holding me, hard and with so much care, I knew, it would never let me go.

part **Three**

I wanted to hear everything, but then for a long time I heard nothing. Nothing, and I knew then why some people disappear into libraries or caves or gliders. Why a deaf person who's offered a cure will sometimes say no, this is not a disease. I heard God and when God went away I heard everything, but what I needed to hear all along was just one sound—a baseball falling, fitting into a glove.

The Smile I Forgot
to Say Anything About

I DON'T REMEMBER WHO GOT ME OUT of the pool, or how I got to the place called Graylin, but for a couple of weeks I couldn't hear anything. And I quit talking.

They had me on a suicide watch, so people came in and out of my room all the time—they even watched me in the bathroom—but since we didn't talk, they were like pictures on a television. A doctor with bleary eyes made me sit in a fat circle with a bunch of kids my age. A girl pissed in her dress once while we were there, then she had to get up to leave and the people next to her on the couch ran off to other chairs. One kid, I later found out was named Freddie, turned over the table in the dayroom and then we didn't see him for a couple of weeks.

After a while, though, things started coming together. I heard what people said, and even talked some. The kid Freddie came back, and then a couple of days later he went up to the nurses' stand and started singing "Amazing Grace" at

223

the top of his lungs. Someone told me he was cheeking his medicine. He went away again, to what they called High Restriction. Graylin wasn't a very happy place, but I wasn't desperate to get out, either. I earned privileges, which meant I could go around without an escort.

The kid, Freddie, smoked, and when he got out of Restriction, we'd go around behind the cafeteria and have cigarettes. He said it couldn't hurt us if we quit before we were eighteen. "I'm quitting everything then anyway," he said. "What the fuck's so great about being old?" We found a couple of matchbox cars in the woods behind the cafeteria one day and we started going out to make roads, build bridges, around this stream. He kept looking behind him, like someone would catch him for being fourteen and still playing with toys. We even made the sounds, car crashes, we couldn't help it.

My mom came to see me at Graylin. We were about three hours from Seattle, in some mountains, and after a few months it was getting cold. She brought me boots and gloves and a warm coat, all brand-new, and everything fit just right. She showed me articles she'd written—they were beautiful, she'd seen so many places and people, I wished I could have gone with her. She said I wouldn't recognize Carson, she was a peach, but she was too young to visit. Frankie came once, but I could tell from how she hugged me that it was hard for her.

I thought about my dad, too. It was the first thing I thought of every morning. I considered he might even be dead or in prison. I almost asked my mom, but I didn't. For a long time after I got to Graylin I would hear his voice at night, just behind my ear, so real it made me jump. And if he was really alive, I secretly wished he was thinking about me too, that maybe there was an empty chapel wherever he had run away to and he'd go there and wonder if I was fine. Or, I tried to remember the trip, the gun, the speeding, not knowing if he'd really tried to kill me. But when I realized what I was thinking, it was like sharp bits of my bones were floating around inside me. I learned not to think about that so much.

I gained six pounds. The other kids started to like me. I even played basketball, and watched movies on TV, and had a pillow fight with Freddie.

It snowed, early. I'd been there a few months, but now it was like it was new. I went outside behind the cafeteria to where I played cars with Freddie.

My foot bumped something. I reached down and brushed away the snow and found one of the cars, the Jeep Wrangler. It was frozen to the ground. I kept kicking it till it came loose, then I picked it up. It was so cold, and small; it didn't seem that small the last time we'd played with it. After I kicked around for Freddie's car for a while, I gave up. Freddie had started to trade the depressed kids cigarettes for their pills. He hadn't wanted to play in a while. I thought about flinging the Wrangler off into the woods. Instead, I stuck it in my jeans' pocket.

I'd been on hikes along the short trails at Graylin, but I hadn't walked anywhere in the snow. One trail led from the school building to the top of the hill behind Graylin, and another went along the ridge a while before heading back down to the dining area. But there was somewhere else—a creek—and I wondered where it started. We weren't supposed to head off into the woods without an escort, and they'd never let us go off the trails. Being in an undesignated area meant losing privileges, and I hadn't lost any since I'd been off the suicide watch.

But I went anyway, along the thin creek, grabbing

branches to steady myself, crunching the snow, sliding now and then just up to the icy water. In some places the rocks in the creek were big enough to step on and I did, even with the ice, then I'd scramble up the opposite bank, my boots losing traction at the steepest part, so I'd have to find something to grab to keep from sliding all the way back down. I made it every time. I breathed the cold air so hard that it stabbed my lungs. Every now and then the trace of a thought would begin fighting its way out, but then I just climbed harder, chose routes along the banks that were thicker with spiky, bare branches. I crouched, ducked, pulled myself along, my hands always reaching for what was just in front of them, my feet always finding holes and thick clumps of grass and buried branches. Like a deer, silently, I climbed.

At the top I found a tree perfect for climbing, but I sat under it instead. It was an evergreen, but not with needles; it had broad, beautiful leaves that held lines of snow along their stem veins. I touched one just over my head, and the snow spilled out, some of it hitting right at the corner of my eye. The stream had disappeared somewhere not too far back, or had started, but I hadn't noticed. I took off my gloves, holding my hands up, the clean air between my outstretched fingers, like I was naked again.

Somewhere a bird probably sang, or a squirrel raced down a tree. The creek, I'm sure, must have babbled not far from where I sat; probably, a car inched down a road nearby, its tires a wet hum along the pavement; maybe, even, another voice called from the hospital, or a house down the other side; or a hunter had popped off a round or two that echoed off some other hill.

But there, it seemed like I only heard what anyone else would have. My lungs took soft breaths now, the steel of the winter air dulled to almost nothing. Nothing but blue, the quiet blue of my own lungs.

"Levi Revel, someone to see you." Elva McCartney chirped over the PA. "Oh Mr. Revel, come out, come out, wherever you are." She was about thirty pounds overweight, but it looked good on her. I was playing Risk in the dayroom. The first month at Graylin I didn't play, then one day I came up to the table and watched. No one invited me to pull up a seat and I didn't. The next day I pulled up a seat anyway and they played me in. I hardly ever won, which for a while made everyone talk to me like I was stupid, like I couldn't hear them. But I'd been playing for a few months now, at least two hours every day, and I had a particular strategy that no one had guessed. In fact I was able to win as much as anyone else, and that helped me talk more.

"Hey Levi, you know what I think," said Bull, a little fifteen-year-old who laughed when he wasn't supposed to, "they found out you been jerking off, is what. They gonna take you to a place up on a mountain and stick electric shocks in you—"

"You would know, Bull," Freddie said. He actually liked Bull, but he ragged on him. Bull's leg always shook. "Too bad they forgot to unplug you when they got done."

They waited for me to leave. Freddie acted like he was going to steal one of my armies. "I know where everything is," I said. "Touch one of my armies and I'll tell McCartney you cheek your Haldol."

"Aren't you a bad motherfucker," Freddie gnawed at his thumb.

"Don't say motherfucker, Freddie." I shook my finger at him, then laughed. "I'll bet anyone at this table ten dollars that it's another doctor out there to see me." I stroked my chin, like a doctor deep in thought. I made my voice low. "Can you tell me what day it is? Who is the president? Where can we contact your father?"

I leaned toward them, whispering. "I think I've got a good one this time. If he starts in with a bunch of questions, here's what I do." I glanced behind me. "I tell him that there's a guy in the Army who wants to kill me. A real tough guy, like six foot four, and this guy can shoot the cap clean off a Coke bottle from a hundred yards, not even chip the glass. He could live in the middle of the desert or in a cave as long as he had to. And I got to find him first, cause I know all about some of his evil secrets." Bull's eyes were riveted to my hands, like I was hiding a knife, waiting for an attack. I leaned closer to him. "So, I say, Doc, see, I'm just trying to keep us all from getting hurt." I snapped my fingers and Bull gasped.

Freddie touched one of my armies. I smacked his hand, harder than I meant to, and it sounded across the room. "And if you don't believe me," I said, "I'll tell you just what kind of secret—"

Elva McCartney stood huge over the table where we sat, her hand suddenly waving in front of my face. "Hello? Hello down there." She was kind in a way that only someone who's overweight can be kind, it came out of her skin. They always called her when a kid wouldn't leave his room, or threw a chair, or hit a staff member.

"He's not on your authorized visitor list, sweetie." The faintest concern showed on her brow. "He says—he says he came a long ways. The gal at the front desk told him no, but he made her call back to ask you." She whispered *Everest Revel* into my ear. I started. "You can say no," she said.

"It's okay," I nodded. She went back to her station and picked up the phone.

"You're fucking white as a sheet, dude," Freddie said reverently. "What's going on?"

The doors to the hall clanged open. When my dad walked in, taller and heavier than anyone we'd seen before on the fourth ward, with his shoulders stretching across the hallways, his black hair uncut and wild, his jeans tattered and tight across his thighs, with his heavy tan boots hitting the floor, and his eyes, in this place where every pair of eyes was broken, with his eyes boiling with a ferocity that did not seem human, the very air of the place went wild. Bull let out the tiniest breath, rolled his eyes back into his head, and fell slowly from his chair to the floor. Freddie didn't move to help him.

"I need you for something." Even though my dad spoke quieter than I'd ever heard him, his voice overwhelmed the dayroom. A familiar dampness came again to my hands, and it flashed before me that it might not be my dad after all, that it might be just one of the voices, a hallucination like Freddie would have.

Then my dad's hand came to my shoulder, so gently. "It's me," he said. "Your dad."

A commotion stirred up behind me. Elva had rushed to Bull, and was patting his face. Bull's eyes were open now, and he was trying to sit up.

"I know, Dad. We should go." I waved to the hallway. He took an awkward step; his knee almost went out from under him. He had changed, even more than I realized—shocks of white-gray hair swept back from his temples, and his mouth didn't close in a hard line but was pulled crooked, into a confused scowl. His eyelids were thin and red.

We went into the parking lot. He seemed lost. "This place," he said, an old-man tenderness to his voice, "do you want out of here? Do you want me to take you out of here?"

I stopped. "What happened to you?"

He reached into his shirt pocket for a cigarette, but it was empty. Still, he kept fishing around for a while before he gave up. "I was driving around," he waved one hand nowhere in particular, "and I was thinking about when you were a kid, when you'd preach from up on the roof of the house, do you remember that?"

I nodded.

"And I used to listen to you from inside the house and think, that boy is going to say the right words to somebody someday, he's going to be a great preacher or teacher." He was talking like every word was costing him. "I was just thinking about that," he said.

We stood a while then, like we were listening to each other.

"I'll be going, then," he said. He pressed a roll of bills into my hand.

There may have been words I should have said then. What if, I wondered, he'd just been in prison, or if he hadn't talked with anyone for all those months? What if he came to me because of something I'd said on a roof somewhere, something about God or love or being saved, and he'd wanted to hear it again? I would have said whatever he wanted, I decided later, if I'd known what it was.

If I'd seen him on the street, I would have probably thought he was just some loser, some guy who had done some things wrong, and it was too late to put them back right. That was the last I saw of him, and since then I've been sorry about that too. He's only in one picture I have, and that's just the one side of his face. But it's a good side. You can see the way he was when he was building our house in Michigan, with the hard lines of his nose and jaw and eyebrow, and shadows everywhere, but then, a little closer, there's the corner of a smile, the smile I forgot to say anything about.

The Only Thing Left

A FEW MINUTES AFTER HE DROVE OFF, I hopped the fence around Graylin. It was just chain link; that was one of the first things I'd noticed, that it was the kind of fence that would work for people who they thought would kill themselves, but not people they thought would kill someone else. I walked to the bus station. I went straight to the bathroom and took off my shirt and washed myself. I had a gash over my eye, where I'd scratched myself on the fence, and it was swelling up so I rubbed soap in it. It looked like it might leave a scar, a scar that would look good. The bathroom smelled like an old mint. A man came in and washed his face in the next sink and watched me in the mirror. I paid a quarter and went in a stall and sat down and pulled three bills from my sock. The sock was dirty and smelled like a man's.

I went up to the counter and bought a bus ticket for forty-five dollars. The guy at the counter handed me a piece of paper with runaway hotlines on it. I left it. Then I crossed the street to an outdoor shop that sold tents and gear and I bought different clothes than I had ever had on my body. In the dressing room I saw myself in the mirror again, saw the cut over my eye and the whiteness of my skin. I saw that I needed underwear too. I tried on pants with cargo pockets and saw how they looked in the front and from the back and from each side. I tried on shirts with the names of companies on the front. I saw how they looked from every angle. I had seen other boys wearing those kind of clothes, that it made them look good and the clothes made me look good too. They were not cheap. Including two pairs of thick socks, three pairs of underwear, a belt, a camp-style wristwatch, a small duffel bag, a pocket first-aid kit and a pocket knife, the two shirts, a sweatshirt, and the pair of pants, it cost a hundred and ninety-two dollars cash. Outside, I shoved my old clothes into a city trashcan on the sidewalk.

It was still three hours until the bus so I ate at the counter in the bus station. I had coffee and bought the first pack of cigarettes I'd ever bought, a red pack of Pall Malls. The waitress who gave them to me asked if I was old enough, but she asked it like a joke. She was a kid herself. I asked her for three books of matches. I tapped the pack against the heel of my hand and opened it, lit one, and looked back at her. She was pretty, to me at least, because of how the light broke in her eyes. She brought me coffee even though my cup was full. My clothes were fitting better than anything I'd ever had on my body. I smoked two cigarettes right in a row, and it made me dizzy. I thought about my dad, about watching him walk off, how he'd put the money in my hand when he left, like he knew that there were some things that only four hundred dollars could solve.

There was still another hour before the bus would come. I went to the ticket counter and asked for six dollars in quarters and I called Frankie's. Carson answered the phone. I told her that I was taking a bus trip, in case Graylin called our mom trying to find me. Carson asked did I run away and I said no, it was more like not running away. She didn't answer that. She talked so softly I could barely hear her, and some of the time I wasn't even sure she was saying anything. I touched the cut over my eye. She said that Frankie was a person who had learned about living, that they went to a Seattle Mariners' baseball game and ate sausage dogs and hot pretzels with mustard and drank cokes and Frankie let her have a sip of her beer, and that they didn't sit where it said to on their tickets but that Frankie just walked right on down to where she said she could see the way the boys filled out those uniforms and sat right down just like she had brought those seats from home. Carson whispered about a bat boy, about him looking right at her. She asked me something about school and I laughed a little, because when I thought about school, it didn't seem like a place that existed anymore. While we talked, I looked out the window of the bus station. Between two buildings I could see the road to Graylin I had just come down. I probably could have just walked away down the road instead of jumping the fence, but someone might have seen me, and started with questions. I knew one thing, that I was done with questions. So I jumped, and cut my eye, but it was worth it.

Carson went on. It was more than she had ever said since before we started building the house in Michigan. She talked to me about things I wanted to hear, about two dogs that Frankie had found, that they had to put one to sleep, but that Frankie was so cool about it, they actually went out to an Italian restaurant to make them feel better, and they had bread that you dipped in oil and then Parmesan cheese. They even ordered escargots, which was now Carson's favorite food in the whole world. Frankie made it a game for them to go into restaurants in Seattle and order nothing but escargots, just to find out which restaurant knew how to do it best.

All the while she talked I looked out at that piece of road, at the waves the sun made off the snow, at the people on the other side of the glass. I thought about what Carson might look like, but I could only think of her with the too-short bangs she got from cutting her own hair that time, that made her look like she was stupid, although I never said that to her. Once or twice I thought I saw a man at some corner that looked like my dad, but I knew better.

Talking to Carson put me at ease, even my stomach calmed down, and I tried another cigarette. She sounded good, I decided. I wondered if Frankie was minding having a kid in her house. They called my bus and I went on. I kept my duffel bag with me, and set it on the seat next to me, but an old lady sat there anyway. She was poor. Her dress pulled apart at the buttons, and she had a paper bag that smelled like mustard. She did not talk to me. She was on the bus a long time but she never got up to use the bathroom, she never got off at stops, she didn't eat a bite of whatever was in her bag. After a while I quit thinking about her and looked a long ways out the window. It would have been good to sleep, but there just was no way. If I did get tired, the smell of the mustard kept me up.

A lady hit her kid three times and said she would throw him out the window. I thought about saying something to her. My mom did that a couple of times that I could remember. She once saw a mother force a screaming kid to go in the waves at Lake Michigan and she walked out in the waves and put her finger in the woman's face and she talked and talked out there in the waves. The woman did come in. When my mom came to sit back down she could not sit. She said that women like that should have their uteruses clamped off.

I bought a magazine at the first stop that told stories about people on television and in the movies and singers and politicians. I didn't recognize hardly any of them, even though they were famous, good and bad, and I wondered why there was so much I didn't know. I had heard some of the names but I had never heard of the movies or television shows or teams or things that they did, or why what they were doing was so important.

There did not seem to be anything happening wherever we drove. I had to think because I couldn't sleep and the old woman next to me had started sleeping, and there was nothing happening when I looked out the window except what I'd already just seen. I turned things over in my mind, my mom and dad, and Carson.

They were somewhat sad thoughts, but they worked out slowly enough. Mainly, I guessed, I missed my mom. I thought of hugging her to me when I got there, of doing that the very first thing, and she would kiss me, I knew she would. That was exactly what she would do.

I bought a pad of sketch paper and two pencils when the bus stopped the next time. I had to go across the street to get it and they had to sharpen the pencils for me so I almost missed the bus. I didn't sit near the old woman now, but I could still smell her mustard. When I laid my head against the window to try to sleep, just as my eyeballs turned heavy, I would start awake. I took out the paper. I never drew much, but now I wanted to.

I wasted several sheets of the sketch paper. There was nothing to draw. The things out the window went by too quickly. There was an old man about three seats in front of me, with white curly hair and red skin. He had a profile. But when I tried to draw it, it looked stupid, too big. I drew a vase with flowers. The flowers looked flat. I wadded the paper in the seat beside me. The floor of the bus was sticky. The bus driver never looked back. A woman behind me started talking to someone about how much she used to drink, how she got kicked out of her apartment once because a guy she didn't even know punched a hole in every wall of the apartment. No one was answering her. She sniffed a lot when she talked.

I finally sat up and lit one of the Pall Malls. The lights in the back of the bus were dimmed and almost everyone now was sleeping. When I got up to use the bathroom in the back of the bus I took the wads of paper with me, holding them in my arm like a baby. After I rested a while longer, I thought I had an idea of what to draw. It was nothing much, I knew, it did not have any meaning in it, no wrinkled faces, no one dying one way or another, no crosses, no deep eyes, no hands trying to hold on to something that was about to fall away, no children with want in their bones.

I drew one thing that I'd always wanted, even though I had never thought about wanting it: a beautiful car. Exhaust pipes came down the sides and out the back, an air scoop cut into the hood, the wheels just looked fast, low and fast. The mirrored glass hid the inside, but I drew that too, in a corner of the page: the serpentine dashboard, Corvette dials, a trim console. It was called the Black Widow Spyder, in letters that looked like wind was blowing over them. In my lap, while I finished the last details of the car, the paper that only an hour and a half ago had been as white as every other sheet now held a car that I had fallen in love with, a car that had been lurking, parked in the back of my mind for years. This was it: every detail was perfect, from the cat-muscle shape to the slight spoiler that finished it off.

Growling, it found a road. We drove deserts, the long straight hundred and sixty mile an hour stretches between nothing towns, the sand whipping into clouds three stories high behind us. I tore along rocky mountain roads, crossing lanes to take the inside curves. Through Michigan, past orchards and cornfields in the cool sunlight, over the sand of the Florida Panhandle, the wheels flying out from under me. The engine whined, the wheels caught. I took it over long bridges, in the green Appalachian Mountains, and crawled through city streets at night, the streetlights making mirrors of the wet road. It was impossible to be alone in such a car, with the green dials and the black leather and the solid hammer of the gearshift. People all over the country stopped walking to see me go by, they looked out restaurant windows, men who were working held their shovels and hammers still.

I drove away, faster and faster across every road I'd lived on, through the towns, past the schools and churches, never stopping for gas, or to eat, or sleep. Then I drove away from those places, to the places I'd heard that other people sometimes went, Chicago, Traverse City, Panama City, Phoenix, Yosemite, Disneyland, ballparks, small colleges, graveyards, places advertised on billboards and arcades. I saw the country from the snow to the swamps. I took in what I'd missed every other time, and I listened to the music I'd heard kids talk about in school at lunch or even at church after Sunday School, Viper and the Tragic Choices, Hella Blue, Rain on Mary's Parade. When I'd seen it all through my windows I finally stopped, eating Big Macs and Taco Bell Grandes, sitting through movies where women's breasts filled the screen, buying souvenir keychains, and stickers for my rear window, riding a roller coaster at a county fair, sneaking into a baseball game and eating sausage dogs.

More Like Not Running Away

———

I remembered that time, that time I'd had my hands on the steering wheel and my dad's legs moved the pedals and we made lazy circles in his truck across that field, I don't even think we were on a path, we just rolled over the tall weeds, and insects drifted out of our way. It wasn't really even those words, Easy cheetah, it wasn't the smell of his cigarettes or even having my hands on the wheel. Now I think it was nothing but a moment, a moment when I couldn't even see his face, but I knew he was smiling. I'm sure of it.

When the bus came to the outskirts of Seattle, I folded the sketch and slipped it into my duffel bag. My new clothes did not feel clean anymore, and I thought I should buy a toothbrush at the bus stop. I did, and I splashed water on my face. I went into a stall and put on clean underwear and socks and threw the dirty underwear and socks into the trashcan even though I'd only worn them once. I bought another pack of Pall Malls even though I still had some left from the old pack, and it felt good when the man handed me the fresh pack, with the cellophane wrapper so tight and the pack not crumpled at all.

I ran to a gift shop next door to the bus station. I wanted a gift for my mom, something that would make her think about me like she used to. Not a necklace, or bracelet. I saw a paperweight at the counter, a thick clear plastic cube with a Bible verse printed on a little scroll frozen in the plastic. It said *For God so Loved the World that He sent His Only Begotten Son that Whosoever Believeth in Him shall not Perish but have Everlasting Life.* As I paid the four dollars, I remembered that it was not one of my mom's favorite verses even though the pastors quoted it all the time. But she wouldn't hate it either.

I thought again of my dad. He had said once that he could

never be caught unless he wanted to be caught, that he knew how to disappear completely. I wondered, if I ever had to disappear myself, how I would do it. I thought about that for a long time, for hours it seemed, until I finally caught a cab to take me to Frankie's house. Well, I thought, I hadn't been able to come up with anything. It might not be a thing someone could ever know, how to disappear completely, until the time came when that was the only thing left to do.

Duval asks me did anybody get killed after all. *I think maybe I've said more than I should, that he's sick of hearing me. Or maybe he doesn't believe me, that all this really happened. Maybe he thinks my dad just had a bad temper, that I was seeing everything worse than it really was.*

My dad did write me a letter that I keep folded in a book. It came to my dorm at Chapel Hill. I waited till I got to my bed to open it and then I lay down to read it. He spelled easy words wrong, he didn't use periods or commas or capitals. But I could see that he took his time with every letter. He said he was proud that I was at college. He told me to work hard, to dress for class. He said he wanted to come see me, that things were getting better now, that he missed me. I wished he could have called—I wanted to tell him that I was playing intramural baseball, that I'd hit a double, and caught a line drive.

I haven't heard his voice for so many years now, it might have gotten a lot softer than I remember. And he would be surprised to hear me, my voice, how much it's changed.

Duval's taught me a lot. People who climb, he says, have to trust the ropes, and they really have to trust the person who anchors the ropes. That's what I try to remember, that just one moment of turning away means I could fall, or make someone else fall. So I hang on, all the time.

A Garden Alone

I GOT INTO THE CAB, but when the driver asked where I was going, I realized I didn't know the address. I knew a Motel 6 was close by, so I told him we might have to drive around for a little while until I recognized a street. He made me show him that I had money to pay. I looked for something I recognized, and thought about how to tell my mom why I wasn't still in the hospital like I was supposed to be. The difficulty lay in what not to say and how not to say it. It would be hard to talk to her without almost crying. No, I thought, no, this all makes sense and I have to act like I'm supposed to be here, like my dad never stopped by the hospital. *I don't want to say anything, really,* I would say, *except that things are different now, this time things are really different,* and then her arms would wrap around me. Even if we cried, we would leave the crying behind us and wake up the next day and have a pot of coffee and plan about all the things we could do next, if we wanted.

More Like Not Running Away

I took the plastic Bible verse out of my pocket and left it on the seat of the cab. I wished I had bought a necklace.

The cab cost eighteen dollars plus two for a tip. It didn't take too long to find Frankie's; I remembered I could see the baseball stadium from it. When I got out, I tucked in my shirt. The new clothes would surprise my mom; I knew they looked good, and that they were good quality. She liked me to look nice, even though some of the clothes she picked for me to wear, crew-neck sweaters and plaid shirts, always made me look too skinny and pale. It did feel like I had been gone for years, and I wondered if I would look older to her. I tried to open a downstairs back door. The door stuck, swelled up with water because it was not protected by any roof. A design flaw, my dad would say. I started to kick at it, but I remembered my mom's hand over mine once before. "Just a little with your foot is all it takes," she'd said. "Don't yank things. Just because it's not ours doesn't mean we can't take care of it like it was." I nudged it.

"Mom?" I listened for her. The quietness made me stop. The top edge of the baseboards of Frankie's townhouse had been wiped clean. The floor shone, smelled faintly of pine cleaner. My mom might be reading a newspaper. She would laugh at something, and say *There is nothing as strange in our house as what is stranger somewhere else.*

No answer still. I called again, but not as loudly. I went to the living room and dropped my duffel bag. I walked down a hall and saw what I figured was Carson's room and recognized one of my books on top of the dresser. I walked in. There were clean sheets on the bed. I touched the top of the dresser; it had an oily shine, no dust even under the pictures. Just as I opened the first drawer, I knew what I would find. My shirts, the ones I'd left in Florida, were folded, but not just like usual, they were folded the way I liked them, the way they folded shirts in the store. All my old socks and underwear were clean. I thought for a moment I might put them on, but I stopped. They had the rest of my books, too, my shoes, some notebooks, a pocketknife. It was weird to see my things in a strange place, like I was an amnesiac just now remembering who I'd been.

I had to see my mom first. I remembered the drawing of the car and went back into the living room and took it out of my duffel bag. It had wrinkled, but I took it anyway. I went by the kitchen. "Mom?" I didn't call loudly. I poured myself a glass of tap water. One of my old drawings, of a barren tree, was unfurled and clamped to the fridge door. Against the pure white door, the tree looked like a gash with dozens of cracks leading from the trunk.

The townhouse was cold. When I walked out of the kitchen it even made me shiver. At a window I stopped and looked to the tiny back yard. The bushes needed cutting. That was something I could do right away. Even if they weren't home, I was sure I could find some shears and get started, and then when everyone got back the first thing they would notice was the how the bushes were trimmed. Things like that would be different now. Now we'd all notice details like that, we'd all be able to keep things neat and orderly.

I had the idea that I might take them all out to a dinner with the money I had left. I could only remember a couple of times being in a restaurant with my mom, but that day I thought we'd sit at a table with her and Frankie and Carson and have some coffee and slices of cake from the glass cases.

"Mom, I'm home." There was only one room I hadn't been to. The door, to her room, was not shut all the way. As I reached to open the door, as my hand touched the metal of the knob, as I tried to take a breath, the breath did not go down right.

Sometimes, when I'd go to a new school, I'd pretend that I didn't have a mother. I even tried it a few times, to see if I could make a little lie like she did—I would get talking to some kid and he'd say something about my mom and I'd shake my head and say "I lost my mom." Just that easy. In the emptiness of the townhouse, just before I opened her door, I saw that if someone really did lose a mother, it would be just like this. It seemed I'd heard of a hundred different ways in a hundred different places that mothers had gone, gnawed away by a slow cancer or taken through the windshield of a rolling car or just by running away. But losing a mother had to mean never going home again.

Of course I knew she might not be there.

But I had not thought until I touched that doorknob that my dad might have gotten there before me. That she could be crouched over in a corner, a single bullet clean in her chest. Or that he'd taken her with him, to make her say she loved him before he killed her and himself. I imagined other things, terrible to think about—had I seen an empty prescription bottle by the sink? One of the kids at Graylin never talked a single word, but we heard that his mother had killed herself, that he'd come home from school one day and there she was, she'd cleaned the whole house and then died.

The emptiness of the townhouse cried back at me. The Lysol hanging in the air stung my nose. The stinging took my throat and eyes, sharper and sharper, and it took my breath.

I opened her door. Two packing boxes were along the wall by her closet.

I put my face between the dresses in her closet. I wrapped

the empty sleeves around my neck. I breathed in a loneliness so deep that it bent the air like an absent ghost. It was her loneliness, sinking into me the way they say the tongues of fire sank into people's souls at Pentecost. I'd always known, in one place in my throat, how Jesus must have cried in the garden—crying not to die, because there was no fear of death, and not to leave his friends, because he walked alone, and not to suffer, because the blood and bruises and thorns were part of his perfection—but crying because he could not find his father's face, because when he would suffer all that he could bear, the pain of every person, living and dead, in that dark moment, there was really nobody there.

And here I was, with the mental hospital still one thought away from whatever else I was thinking, kneeling in my mother's closet, but not to pray. I wanted tears to sting in my eyes. I knew there should be tears somewhere from everything that had happened to me, that I should be weak and things should all be spinning, but I saw everything so clearly, the colors and textures of the cottons and linens, the brown and black empty hangers. The air was thick with mothballs and shoe leather, and distant cigarette smoke.

I waited and waited, even as the shadows came over more and more of the room. I waited, wanting to move, wanting her hand to find me asleep there, to touch my head. But after a while, I went out into the kitchen and poured myself a glass of cold milk.

They were not gone long. When they all came home I was at the kitchen table. They rushed to me, and threw their arms around me, and never asked about why I was there. They all talked at once, their words tumbling gently, wrapping me tight, but not too tight. I heard them, each voice, each word, and it all made sense. Carson was so tall, there was hardly any little girl left in her. She held my hand while she talked, telling me about some girls who always wanted to see this picture she had of me, and Seattle and coffee and the Mariners.

"You should play baseball," she said. "Now that you're home."

There was a pool for the townhouses outside, I could see through the window behind Carson. Some kid was walking along just sticking the toe of his shoe in the water. It had to be freezing. His mom came up from behind him and pulled him away.

"Mom," I said at last, "what are we going to do?"

She looked away from me for just a moment, to a place in the room where there wasn't anything. When she turned back to me, I saw something I'd forgotten, from so long ago, before we'd moved too many times, when she would still come to my room at night to pull the sheets up to my chin, when she would kiss each of my eyelids. "What*ever*," she said, giving her head a little wobble, her shoulders a funny shrug. Everyone looked suddenly to everyone else, our mouths all held in slack O's. Then the laugh hit us all at once, a good hard laugh, one that would come back for weeks afterwards, and always right after that exact, perfect silence.

The Author

Nicole Myhre

Paul Shepherd

is a graduate of UNC–Chapel Hill and UNC–Greensboro, and earned a PhD with Distinction from Florida State University, where he was a Kingsbury Fellow and is currently a Writer in Residence. He has also written a book of poetry. His work has appeared in numerous magazines, including *Prairie Schooner, Omni, Portland Review, The Quarterly, Fiction,* and *St. Anthony Messenger.* His community service activities include serving as President of Rainbow Rehab, a nonprofit construction company that rehabs older homes for sale to low-income homeowners, working with family ministries at St. Stephen Lutheran Church, and helping found the House of Mercy, an AIDS hospice in Belmont, North Carolina. He lives in Tallahassee, Florida, with his wife Lois, and children Max, Summer, and Charlie.